The Altered Adventure

Volume One
Secrets of the Cyclone

By
Gary Merritt
(Also known as Gizzy Gazza)

Chapter One

Surviving A Cyclone

Gizzy woke with a headache and tried to focus his eyes. Everything was hazy, though he realized he was no longer in his lounger on the deck of the cruise ship that had been lulling in the Bay of Mexico. He had fallen asleep to the soft music playing in the background, or was it the sound of the gentle waves lapping against the pristine hull?

When his eyes focused, he realized he was on a beach. But, where? The ship had taken off from Galveston, Texas, but he felt really far away now. He vaguely remembered sensing static in the air and the warmth of blowing winds. Thunder! He remembered the loud claps. And huge gusts of wind. Had there been some kind of storm? He shook his throbbing head. He couldn't quite remember.

He sat up and looked around. Gizzy could feel sand in his long, black dreadlocks, so he closed his eyes and shook his hair out. When he opened his eyes again, he scanned the crystal waters. Perhaps he had washed up on a beach in Mexico. He tried to imagine how he would explain it to the locals: "One minute I was lounging on a delightful cruise, and the next minute I got swept away in a cyclone and washed ashore. Could someone take me back to America, please? I imagine they're missing me in Houston right about now!"

But in all seriousness, there was another thing bothering him. He really *did* have a vague memory of relaxing with an ice-cold lemon and lime, and just as he was about to take the first sip, the ship was hijacked by…a band of wild-eyed pirates! It seemed crazy to him even now, but the memory started to come on strong. The pirates had turned out to be his old friends from high school, and he could distinctly remember seeing the faces of Hugh, Brandon, and Clayton.

But could his friends have really commandeered the cruise ship? And why did he feel as if no one else was on the ship when the pirates arrived? Weren't there lots of people aboard when he first got on? And hadn't he seen dozens more file up the ramp and onto the deck? Huh. It was strange thinking of some of his former best friends from high school as part of a pirate gang. While it was true that recently Hugh, Brandon, and Clayton had made a lot of mistakes and chosen a darker path, it still didn't add up.

Gizzy felt a little dizzy and sat back down. He closed his eyes and thought of Clayton. Losing his best friend had hurt Gizzy a lot.

Clayton, or "Cib" as Gizzy called him, had been Gizzy's best friend for ten years. They had met on the first day of preschool at the activities table, molding multicolored Play-Doh into volcanoes and frogs and raptors and any climby, flighty, swimmy, crawly beast they could imagine. They giggled while molding the funny creatures and bonded over their love of the weird and the unknown.

Several years later, when Gizzy was twelve years old, his father ran off with a stewardess from Dallas. No warning. No letter. No goodbye. He just vanished like a wisp of smoke. Gizzy turned to Cib for support. They played in the woods near Cib's house, building forts out of fallen branches and long wild grass. Cib did his best to keep Gizzy laughing and distract him from the deep loss. Gizzy's mother was so devastated that she turned to drinking and became an overnight alcoholic. First it started with several glasses of wine a day. Then an entire box. Then two bottles. Gizzy didn't know what to do, except to try his best to be there for her and take care of her when she needed him.

When Gizzy was a sophomore in high school, he tried to confront his mother and convince her that she needed help. She claimed she wasn't an alcoholic because, as she had put it, "Alcoholics don't drink wine." Gizzy disagreed. Soon his mother had switched to drinking a bottle of whiskey a day, often taking it so far that she would throw up on the carpet or the linoleum and pass out with an empty bottle in her hand or lying nearby.

Gizzy's grades had started slipping. He missed most of his classes because he had to stay home and take care of his mother. It got so bad that even when he did make it to class, he couldn't concentrate; all he could do was think of different ways to help her—buying her mineral water and Ibuprofen, keeping her out of fights with the neighbors, getting her to the next AA meeting. Finally, he decided to sacrifice his education and dropped out of school at the age of fifteen to take care of her full time. Her welfare checks kept them afloat, and Gizzy spent many days and nights hoping to the greater forces of the world that he had the strength to save her. He had always been afraid to seek outside help because he had worried that if anyone found out how poor her condition was that he might be taken away from his mother, and he didn't want to imagine what would become of her if she lost her son, too, and not just her husband.

Cib was worried for Gizzy because he never made it out of the house. He hated seeing Gizzy rot away at home, so he got him involved in a local youth club called T4T, or Teens for Teens, that would meet twice a week. The club would often go mini golfing or grill out at the park. Sometimes they'd go cosmic bowling, and Gizzy would be absorbed by the darkness, mesmerized by the aqua bowling balls and laser lights, fantasizing that he was in a different place, a new world where the hurts and pains of life back home didn't exist.

T4T was a great escape for Gizzy, especially because he could spend quality time with Cib. That was the case until…Brandon joined the youth club.

Brandon was trouble.

He was a charming kid often recognized by his sleek blond hair. He had been kicked out of high school for having been suspended too many times for harassing other students, getting into fistfights, and stealing office supplies from the teachers' lounge. Brandon had a really bad streak in him, which only got worse when he became close friends with Hugh.

Hugh was nineteen and had already graduated from high school. He came from a wealthy oil family and was good at water sports and being an all-around jerk. Shortly after graduation he took a month-long boating course and earned his license with ease. On weekends he would throw huge boat parties with strobe lights, blasting hip-hop music, and lots of alcohol. Hugh's money and brash attitude, along with Brandon's smooth talking and manipulative ways, eventually seeped into Cib like a bad virus. In no time, Cib was partying day and night, ditching classes, getting into fights, and not responding to any of Gizzy's texts or phone calls.

Gizzy felt shut out and alone. He felt like the only fifteen-year-old in the world who truly, really, definitely needed a vacation. Bad. And not just some regular vacation. An *adventure*. Something to take his mind off the harsh realities life had dropped in his lap at such a young age.

Sometimes the world listens.

Out of nowhere, Gizzy received an envelope in the mailbox. It was odd, because he rarely received mail. He excitedly tore open the envelope and found two tickets for a cruise leaving from the Gulf of Mexico. The letter said he had been entered into a raffle through one of the many T4T events, and he had won! Gizzy ran to his mother's room and shook her awake with the good news. His mother was so drunk she could barely speak, and when Gizzy showed her the tickets, she grabbed them and tried to rip them up, mumbling something about how they weren't going anywhere. She was fine being a shut-in.

At the sight of his mother rolling around in the bed and trying to tear the tickets apart, Gizzy completely lost his composure. He had done so much for his mother, and he only wanted this one thing, this small break from his difficult life, from her demanding ways, and she refused. Flat out.

Gizzy's pale face turned beet red. He lunged at her and fought her for the tickets. When he finally pulled one from her, he told her that he hated her and wished she would just drink herself to death already. Then he quickly made some sandwiches, grabbed his sleeping bag, threw on his gray jacket, and took off out of the house.

He spent the next few days hitchhiking from Houston to Galveston, sleeping on benches, showering at rest stops, drinking from the water fountains at local parks, and rationing his peanut-butter-and-jelly sandwiches. Gizzy made it in time for the cruise and convinced the cruise-line worker with the clipboard in front of the boarding dock that Gizzy's mother had left something in their car in the parking lot and was coming right behind. With the long line of people waiting to board the ship, the worker let Gizzy go through and put a checkmark next to his name.

Back on the unknown beach, Gizzy opened his eyes. He dug his white high-top sneakers into the sand and stood up again. What had happened to the pirates? Had they been real or just a figment of his imagination? And how had he survived the cyclone, if that's what it really was?

Gizzy walked around the beach and soon started to notice something odd about the trees. They were…different. He blinked a few times and shook his head. The trees all had thick blue trunks and branches. Blue? How could this be? And the leaves were transparent. Was this some kind of sick, elaborate prank?

He continued to walk around, baffled by the blue trees. Wait a minute. If he had survived the storm and landed safely on the beach, then where was the wreckage from the boat? Shouldn't there be pieces of wood bobbing on the water, twisted metal sticking out of the sand?

Questions flew through Gizzy's mind until he suddenly felt ill and ran to the shoreline where he vomited into the ocean. Gross. He must have been finally feeling the effects of being tossed around by the violent cyclone. A psycho cyclone. Yeah, that was it.

He wiped his mouth on the sleeve of his jacket and finally realized that his clothes weren't even wet.

Wait a minute.

So he had just survived a psycho cyclone, been hurled off a brand-new cruise ship somewhere in the Gulf of Mexico, and found himself on an island full of enormous blue trees where his clothes weren't even wet? Riiiiight.

Gizzy patted himself down one more time just in case. Yup. All dry.

"Hello?" he called out, hoping for an answer.

Nothing.

Gizzy was alone, lost, and unsure of what to do.

"Anybody?"

Nothing again.

Clearly there was no one around. Gizzy felt hopeless and feared his wish for adventure had come true in a way far beyond what he had hoped or imagined. Would he now have to learn how to survive in the wild? Man, if only he had paid more attention when he was watching those survival shows and wildlife documentaries while cooking pasta for his mother.

But he couldn't remember anything from the shows, and they certainly didn't teach wildlife survival in high school. Sure, they taught the boring and pointless mathematics and English and reading skills that lead people to become accountants and secretaries and librarians.

Like any of that was going to help him now.

Then again. Maybe he could somehow use algebra to create some kind of floating craft out of blue tree branches. He could pass the time by singing famous lines from Shakespearian plays...if he could remember any. That ought to scare away the wildlife, if there was any.

Curse you, algebra!

Gizzy's heart started beating faster. What if a wild animal jumped out and attacked him? What if he couldn't find food? What if...

He suddenly heard a movement in the distance. Gizzy put a hand above his eyes and squinted. What was that? Far off, he could see a bunch of ridiculously long yellow leaves shaking. They were attached to rounded bushes sitting on black stumps.

All of a sudden, out ran...a pig. Yup. Just a normal pig. No oddly colored legs or tail or snout. Just a regular old pink pig roaming through the weirdo jungle.

Gizzy slowly walked toward the pig, who hadn't seemed to notice his presence. He crouched as he took deep steps in the sand, which started to fill up his high-tops. Annoying! In his hunched state, he hoped the pig wouldn't see him coming.

When Gizzy got close enough, he hid behind one of the thick blue trees and prepared to jump out, thinking he might be able to catch the pig by surprise. But what would he do from there? He had no idea. Only ten minutes into this strange new world and he was already attacking pigs? Sheesh.

Gizzy squatted down low, flexed his lean arms, and prepared to jump on the pig by counting down in his mind. It was now or never.

Three…Two…One…

"Hello there!" A loud booming voice came out of nowhere, scaring both Gizzy and the pig. The pig, in a state of wide-eyed panic, suddenly grew a pair of black wings and quickly flew away toward the horizon.

Gizzy's jaw dropped. Pigs can…*fly?* And quite majestically, apparently.

Gizzy ran forward and fell in the sand. He quickly got up, shook himself off, and backed up until he hit a tree trunk, his fists up and ready to duke it out if he had to. They sure didn't teach boxing in high school, either!

He looked around to find whoever was behind the booming voice, but nobody was in sight. He quickly ran back to the edge of the ocean to get a better look at his surroundings. The waves rolled up against his ankles. The flying pig was now a speck on the horizon.

"Hello? Who's there?" Gizzy asked, picking up a rock just in case he had to protect himself. He noticed a hole in the rock and saw a little half-hornet crab, half-ant-looking-thing that let out a loud peeping sound. As the crabant peeped, Gizzy dropped the rock to cover his ears, then kicked the rock into the ocean. Did the crabant say, *Weeeeee* as it flew over the water? Or was Gizzy hearing things?

"It is I...Voice. I am a guardian of Altered known as the Air Guardian."

The booming voice echoed across the beach, but Gizzy didn't see a single person or bug or animal or creature. He turned in circles from the ocean to the beach to the jungle and back. Nothing.

It felt as if the voice was coming out of thin air, like an angel was watching over Gizzy.

"Where are you?" Gizzy cautiously asked.

"I'm just a voice...named, well, Voice. Yes, not very imaginative, I know. And I can see how that could be confusing. It's a long story that I can maybe explain another time. Anyway, I'm here to help you. I see you're lost and confused, and your shoes are full of wet sand. You might want to dump those out soon, or all the sloshing will really start to be a bother. Well. Um. Anyhow. If you have any questions I can answer them for you."

Gizzy thought long and hard before asking anything of the deep voice that was apparently watching over him. Nothing weird about that, right? Although, Voice was right about his shoes.

"Hang on," Gizzy said, and he pulled off each shoe, dumped the gooey sand out, then put his high-tops back on. "Ugh, that sand came out like disgusting old oatmeal."

"Um. I suppose so...although I have no idea what oatmeal is," Voice said. "So, I'm here to help you. Did you think of any other...pertinent questions?"

"You mentioned Altered. What's Altered?" Gizzy asked.

"Altered is the name of this world. You're in Altered, and I'm one of the four guardians who protect it. Myself, Inferno, Letvia, and Ratchet. We're all here to protect you throughout your stay in our world, so please don't be shy if you need anything."

Gizzy still couldn't wrap his head around the idea of being in a different world. Especially one called Altered.

"But…how did I *get* here? I mean, people don't just fall asleep on a cruise ship and wake up in some other random world. Not where I'm from, anyway!"

Silence.

"Um. Voice? Are you still there?"

Gizzy was trying desperately to process everything that was happening. He walked forward a few steps and dropped to his knees. The sand felt cool and grainy on his kneecaps. Would he be stuck in Altered forever?

"Voice, if you're there, can you tell me how I can get back home? I assume you know a planet called Earth? You've maybe seen it from far away. It looks green and blue, and there are some brown squiggles of land. It's two-thirds water, though." Hey, Gizzy remembered something from science class! "Voice, I…I have someone counting on me back home. I said some harsh things to my mom, and, well, it's just that I need to get back and apologize and make things right again. And on top of that, she really needs me! She's not used to functioning without me, and I don't know if she could now."

Again, silence. Gizzy reached his hands into the sand and squeezed fistfuls of it—a thousand tiny stress balls in his grasp. He watched the sand fall from his hands in a waterfall of fine brown grains.

Then he stood up, sighed, and started to walk away toward the jungle.

"There is a way home."

Gizzy stopped and turned around.

"The Prophecy. It can help you get home."

"The Prophecy? What's the Prophecy?"

"I can't exactly tell you."

A rather odd response. What was so bad about the Prophecy that he wouldn't say what it was?

"I'll help you find the Prophecy and get you home."

Gizzy smiled. Finally, some good news in this crazy world! "Thank you! How do I find the Prophecy? Where is it?"

"I'll show you in the morning. It's almost nightfall. You can probably tell by the shifting sky. As someone who has never experienced Altered at night...you really don't want to. Take my word on this one, young man. Now, quickly, there's a shack to the east that'll keep you safe until morning. But be very careful to avoid the quicksand pool when you get there. It's a hundred paces behind the shack, so watch your step. Go. Now! The sky's growing dark!"

Gizzy watched the sunset as it quickly descended beyond the horizon. The sun seemed to drop much faster in this world. He also noticed for the first time that the sun was a deep, deep red. Interesting.

13

Suddenly, Gizzy heard strange noises coming from the jungle. Insects singing and hissing, wild pack animals howling, jaws chomping, and the sluggish sounds of slimy movements. He figured that this strange world would have diverse and different creatures than he had ever known, and whatever lived beyond the blue trees could easily harm him.

But if Gizzy were to take Voice's advice and find the shack, he would have to face those hazardous sounds coming from the jungle. He would have to trust Voice that the shack would be his only safe haven from the lurking creatures. So he gathered all his strength, breathed in deeply, and took off through the jungle.

As he sped through, his legs churning like blurry wheels, he was hit in the face with sticky gray cobwebs and had to knock curling vines away with his fists and forearms. He felt his movement slowing the deeper he went, his sneakers being sucked down by the almost-alive mud holes. He panted hard as he moved through the now-dark planet, a strange green glow in the sky. He could see all colors of eyes looking at him from a distance—pink, yellow, purple, aqua, magenta, orange. And the eyes weren't just in pairs. Single eyes. Triple eyes. Dozen-eyed beings watching this human boy trudge through the jungle at top speed.

Finally, Gizzy saw a clearing and dove. He tucked and rolled along the smooth, cold grass, sprung to his feet, took a look back at the screaming jungle, and continued sprinting. He made sure to run in a wide arc to avoid the quicksand pool Voice had mentioned. Soon Gizzy was at the door of the slanted brown shack. Wow, he didn't even know he had those kinds of moves in him! Thanks, P.E. class!

Before Gizzy went inside the shack, he was able to take some deep breaths and settle himself a bit. He looked into the distance at that green glow that had settled over the darkness. He looked up at the moon; it was green with particle waves flowing out of it like blowing curtains. Holy smokes! The moon in Altered was green!

Gizzy quickly turned around, pulled open the shack door, and ran inside. The one-room space was small, airy, and filled with strange, luminous cobwebs. Gizzy reached toward the ceiling and touched one of the webs; it shimmered on like a lightbulb. Cool!

At one end was a fireplace full of thick, oblong pieces of wood. Gizzy walked cautiously toward the fireplace and looked around for something to light it with. One of his favorite survival shows back home had been *Nowhere Norman's Norwegian Nature Navigation*. Gizzy often saw Norman making fire by rubbing two sticks together, but how would Gizzy make fire with these oblong pieces of wood?

"Here, allow me!" Voice said out of nowhere.

All of a sudden the fireplace shot purple sparks and burst into a brilliant open flame. The light from the fire made the little sanctuary feel safer and much warmer with the fallen night. Gizzy stood near the fire and rubbed his hands together. He looked around for Voice, then remembered he was, well, just a voice. How was he able to create fire out of nothing?

"Wow, thanks, Voice! But…how'd you do that?"

"Like I told you, I'm the guardian of the air."

"But you made *fire*!" Gizzy said, and laughed.

"So I did. Well, this is where I must leave you for now, which means you're on your own for a while. I'll be back tomorrow. Sleep tight, young Gizzy."

"Wait, how do you know my name?"

No answer.

"Voice? Hello? Are you there? I still have questions!"

Voice was clearly gone. Or so it seemed, since Gizzy couldn't see him. He suddenly felt very alone and scared, realizing the gravity of his situation as the fire crackled. He was stuck near a wild jungle, surrounded by bizarre and potentially deadly creatures, and all he had was this fire to keep him safe. A fire he couldn't even start on his own. What a crazy, unexpected adventure.

Gizzy's stomach rumbled. He hadn't eaten anything all day. Now that his nerves were settling a little, he realized just how hungry he really was. At least the light of the fire provided a welcome and comforting glow around the room.

Gizzy had a really bad feeling about all this, and he quickly stood up. He felt he should barricade the door with something heavy just in case one of those crazy monsters tried to break in during the middle of the night. He could faintly hear the howling and buzzing in the distance. Gizzy shuddered. Then he got behind the small bed and pushed it against the shack door, hoping it might somewhat protect him…or at least give him a chance to figure out an escape route if something came knocking.

He found a blanket made from what felt like alpaca wool and laid it down on the old hardwood floor near the fire. Then he curled up on the blanket and shut his eyes. He thought about all the crazy things he'd encountered in this strange new world of Altered—a flying pig, thick blue trees with transparent leaves, half-and-half creatures, a jungle full of the absurd. Oh, and Voice! A being without a body who spoke out of thin air. Quite a memorable experience.

All Gizzy knew for sure was that he needed to survive the night, find this so-called Prophecy, and then make his way home. Would it be really difficult? Did he have what it would take to accomplish his goals? Was his mother doing OK without him? Did she realize he was gone? Did anyone? It felt so lonely lying there on the floor in the small shack. And one other thing was puzzling him; how in the world did Voice know his name?

***

Gizzy had drifted off to sleep while the Altered night took over. Luckily for Gizzy, he was blissfully unaware of the strange and threatening creature lurking in the darkness outside the shack, watching the orange glow of the fire through the window, knowing that a stranger to Altered was sleeping inside. The creature, known as a Green Blood, had the proportions of a human with dry red skin and short white hair, wrinkles all over his body, and large muscles with slick, toned grooves. This Green Blood had black, empty, soulless eyes and clean, straight-cut yellow teeth.

Suddenly, the Green Blood began to produce a siren-like noise from his mouth, talking in a strange language known as Greenbloodian, a language that Gizzy wouldn't possibly know or understand. Very few did. The Green Blood was an extremely rare species that was forced into hiding after the entire group was almost wiped out by the

Bowsmen, a clan that hunted the Green Bloods for their rare and precious skins. Ironically, it now seemed as if the lurking Green Blood wanted to eliminate Gizzy...but what had Gizzy done to upset this creature?

The Green Blood took several steps toward the shack, tensing its muscles and bearing its teeth in preparation for an attack. Just as he was about to reach the door...

"Stop!" Voice's command echoed through the jungle but failed to wake Gizzy. "Stay away from the shack. Do not advance another step, or else."

The Green Blood slowly turned around. "He needs to die," the Green Blood said into the vast sky. "Voice, you said he's going to the Prophecy. That can't happen!"

"Yes, and I'm helping him to the Prophecy. It's the only way! Otherwise, he will never get home. Look, don't worry, Ratchet. I know what I'm doing! Besides, he needs the four keys to open the Prophecy. I'm just taking him to the Prophecy because it holds the power to take him home."

Ratchet believed Voice, as he was commonly thought to be the most honest and trustworthy of the four guardians and was unconditionally loved throughout the Altered world. Ratchet had been recently chosen as a guardian replacement, and for now he would have to trust that Voice knew what he was talking about.

"OK," Ratchet finally said. "But we're all supposed to protect Altered as equals, and I want to do my best as a guardian and give everything I have to keep that promise and protect this world."

"And you're doing a great job so far, Ratchet. You're going to have to trust my word on this one and understand that I have years of experience to speak from. My choices are not arbitrary, and I'm just trying to help the boy get back to his planet. He appeared here through mysterious circumstances, and if you'd plopped into some random world gazillions of lightyears from your own, wouldn't you want to get home, too?"

Ratchet paused in thought. "I suppose," he finally said. He felt a little defeated. "But regardless of what you say, I don't trust the boy. I'll abide by what you say for now, but don't forget that I'm an equal fourth among the powers that be in Altered!"

"Fair enough," Voice said.

"You know, I—"

"Wait, wait," Voice said. He could hear something faint carried on the blowing wind. It was a boy's voice calling out for help. He perceived that it was coming from the ocean waters not too far from where the cyclone had thrown Gizzy. "Ratchet, I know you're upset right now, but another boy needs help. I can hear him calling out far away. He's somewhere near the Julipean beachhead."

"So why are you telling me this?"

"If you want to be looked upon as a good guardian with strength and noble moral character, then go save this boy. After the stunt you tried to pull tonight, it's the least you can do!"

"Daaahhhh!" Ratchet yelled, and then he turned and stormed off toward the jungle.

"It's OK, Ratchet!" Voice yelled, as Ratchet disappeared inside the harsh confines of the dark and howling jungle. "You can always trust me."

However, little did Ratchet know that Voice was, in fact, not telling the truth this time. While it was true that Voice was going to help Gizzy reach the Prophecy, his actual goal was not to send Gizzy back home to Earth. Voice desperately needed to unlock the Prophecy, and he would do everything in his power to ensure that it happened...

Chapter Two

The Being Inside The Beast

As the deep-red sun rose brightly over Altered, Gizzy stirred atop his alpaca blanket and bemoaned a difficult night's sleep. Screeches and growls haunted his dreams, only this time, they had come from the real, outside world, not his imagination.

Purple, flute-like creatures, known as flupleswoops, soared through the morning skies, calling out with their *tee-too-bee tee-too-bee* song as they passed over Gizzy's shack. The fire had died at some point in the night, but the warmth had lasted within the small room. Several scorched, oblong pieces of wood remained in the ash.

Gizzy stood, wiped the sleep from his eyes, and looked out the window. He was thankful he'd survived the night. He watched as the purple creatures flew up and away, their slim tubular bodies shooting through the air at top speeds. Maybe Altered wasn't so bad after all?

Gizzy's stomach grumbled. Man, was he hungry! But he really needed to buckle down and focus on getting back home, and Voice had said he could only do that by making a journey to…what had he called it? Oh, yeah, the Prophecy, whatever that was.

Gizzy moved the bed away from the door. Then he opened the door and stepped outside. Altered actually seemed pretty peaceful in the morning. All he could hear of the jungle in the near distance was a slight, calming buzz.

"Voice. Are you out there?"

No response.

"Voice. Hello? It's Gizzy. I'm tired and super hungry. I haven't eaten in over a day now. Voice. Are you there? I really need to find some food before we do this whole Prophecy thing. I'm guessing there isn't a fast-food joint around here anywhere, huh?" Gizzy laughed at his own joke.

Silence.

Well, shoot! Where did the mysterious voice in the sky disappear to? Wasn't he supposed to lead Gizzy home? He said he would be back tomorrow. Well, it was tomorrow!

Gizzy walked circles around the shack. Over and over. He whistled and hummed and talked to himself. Minutes dragged. The boredom stretched for hours. There was a boulder behind the shack, and Gizzy hopped up on it and sat down. Strangely, the seemingly rigid boulder molded to Gizzy's body, and he found it quite warm and comfortable.

"Thanks. You rock," Gizzy said. He laughed again at his own joke. He wished Cib was there with him. Gizzy knew Cib would have liked his lame joke. Gizzy thought of his mom and his old life. He wondered if she was getting along OK without him, if he would ever have a chance to right his wrong and tell her how sorry he was. She needed him so badly. And Cib. If only he hadn't lost his way. Gizzy had never wanted to let go of him, but what else could he have done? Cib had become a totally different person, like the Cib he had known was unzipped, peeled away, and discarded forever.

Sigh.

Time had dragged, and there was still no sign of Voice. Gizzy looked toward the red sun and watched how it bobbed in the sky. It was certainly different from Earth and something he was trying to get used to. As he looked at the bright crimson light, he started pondering on what things in Altered were similar to his own world. They both had a sun, gravity, oxygen, animate and inanimate life, a concept of time, day and night, and some…kind-of-similar animals. Altered did seem strangely comparable to Earth, though the sun, moon, vegetation, and creatures were definitely, well, *altered*. Almost like Altered was a rough copy of Earth…or Earth was a rough copy of Altered. Either way, the two worlds definitely showed similar makeups.

A loud caw let out from the sky, and a mystical flying beast circled over the shack. It was a giant griffin beating its muscular wings. Gizzy's stomach had been growling for ages, and it signaled to him that he ought to be careful; maybe he was the target of the bird's lunch?

Gizzy sat still within his mold in the boulder and held his breath, hoping for the best. He could see the shadow of the griffin in the grass as it circled and circled, until finally, for whatever reason, it beat its muscular wings a few more times and flew on. Woo! That was a close one.

Well, it was now or never. Gizzy was incredibly hungry, and if he didn't get up and do something about it, he would starve to death or become someone else's…errrrr…something else's lunch. Gizzy knew he had no choice but to walk back into the mighty jungle, so he set off across the clearing toward the blue trees and singing creatures.

The jungle was much tamer in the day. The long, withered vines weren't reaching out for Gizzy, and the winding cobwebs seemed to have disappeared, as if the creatures had sucked them back in. Gizzy searched the ground and bushes for mushrooms, berries, nuts, seeds, or flower petals, but he couldn't seem to find anything to eat. He'd remembered learning in school about native tribes that ate roots and herbs, but how would he know which ones were safe and which were poisonous?

Gizzy's stomach gurgled. He was in dire need of food and water. His mouth felt dry, and his throat was parched. At least the jungle provided shade from the red sun, and there was a cool breeze blowing through the transparent leaves.

Suddenly, he heard a noise in the distance. A rustling. Gizzy crouched down behind an ashen boulder and watched. Some spikey bushes parted and, to his surprise, that same pig that managed to get away from him the evening before was prancing up ahead. Gizzy waited until the pig went by, then he creeped after it, hoping the pig wouldn't escape again.

Tip-toe, tip-toe. Gizzy slunk up behind the happy pig. And just as he prepared to jump the pig (of course, with no idea what he would do once he caught his prey) Gizzy slipped on some slick, transparent leaves and crashed to the ground. The noise startled the pig, and it immediately sprouted its beautiful black wings and took flight in defense.

No! Gizzy watched the pig fly up and away, light as a feather. Then he shook his head, determined not to let it escape again, so he followed his would-be meal. Gizzy chased the pig deeper and deeper into the jungle; he ran for what felt like forever. The pig continued to glide in a straight line just above the treetops like it was taunting Gizzy.

After a while, it appeared as though the pig was getting tired. His pink belly moved in and out at a rapid pace, and he started to glide down. Eventually his wings contracted, and the pig dropped to the ground on all fours, panting so hard Gizzy wondered if he might explode right there on the spot. It probably wasn't every day that a flying pig was chased through the jungle by a human!

Gizzy, also breathing hard, raced toward the pig, and when he finally lunged at him, the pig dodged Gizzy and jumped into a deep, eerie-looking cave that slanted down into the ground. No! He missed him again!

Gizzy picked himself off the ground and ran over to the cave entrance and looked inside. The cave was so dark that it was impossible to see very far in, and he had no clue what dangerous things might be waiting for him inside.

Gizzy stepped back. He was ridiculously hungry, exhausted from running, and his heart was pounding against his sternum. He felt uncertain of everything at this point. Should he really take a risk and see what might be waiting inside the cave? No, probably not worth it. He decided to step back to a safe distance and consider his next move.

So…go inside a freaky, dark cave after the pig or stay out. Gizzy had hidden from the griffin a little while ago and maybe saved himself from becoming the big bird's lunch, so was it worth it now to head into the jagged cave and risk his own hide for a pig he wouldn't even know what to do with? Let alone a flying pig that pranced through the jungle. He decided it wasn't worth probing in the dark unknown by himself. Maybe if Voice ever actually showed up! But not alone.

As Gizzy turned around and started walking away, he heard a blood-curdling screech from the cave. It was the pig! Gizzy kept a safe distance from the cave entrance and breathed heavily. He tried hard to keep himself from hyperventilating. What had caused the dramatic squeal? He figured something inside the cave must have gotten to the pig first...and the pig was probably dead. Gizzy felt a strong sense of relief that he had not suffered the assumed fate of the pig, and as he stepped even farther away from the cave, he had a deep feeling of loss inside him, a guilt about having survived while the pig was presumably gone.

Suddenly, a voice echoed from the cave and made Gizzy shiver throughout his entire body. Was there another human on Altered? A friend or foe? Gizzy stayed at a safe distance, then the mystery being walked out of the darkness and stood at the cave entrance. He was wearing torn clothes, worn shoes, and had bruises all over his dark skin. His brown hair clearly hadn't been washed for a very long time as it looked crusted over and hung in harsh strands. Gizzy wanted to call him a human, but he knew that wasn't quite right. This wasn't a man from Earth, even if he had the proportions of what Gizzy would call a man. But either way, he could tell that this...entity...needed help, or seemed to.

"Please, come. I killed the pig! It's safe inside my cave. We can eat the pig together. You look hungry, young thing! I can tell. I know what hungry looks like. Please, come. It's safe in there. It's more pleasant than you might think."

Gizzy felt unsafe and uncertain. He wasn't sure what to do, but his stomach was taking over, telling him to move toward the cave and the strange being. So Gizzy took slow steps forward, his breaths like little, scared quakes all along the way until he was within ten feet of the being and the entrance.

"Thank you. Um. Yes, I'm hungry. How did you know?"

The being twitched a little. "Oh. As I said, I know what hungry is. I know what it looks like. Nasty. Bad, bad thing."

"Um. Yeah. It's been a while, and I've been trying to find food."

"The pig's in here. Just right this way," the being said, and pointed toward the cave.

"Well, um. So. What's your name?" Gizzy asked.

"Woof. My name's Woof."

Woof? That was an odd name. But maybe it wasn't odd or uncommon in this world. Gizzy needed to remember it wouldn't be like home. Most of this was so new and different. He couldn't expect to recognize anything. He had to keep reminding himself of that. And what was he waiting for? Woof had killed the pig and was offering to share. Then again, why would Gizzy risk going down into a dark and creepy cave just because he was offered free food? Gizzy didn't know Woof. What should he do? He wished Voice had come back like he had promised.

Gizzy's stomach gurgled again and again. It brought a smile to Woof's face. Gizzy slowly stepped back and turned. Then he noticed that the world was beginning to dim. Oh no! Did they have shorter days here? Was the length of the days random and varied? He could feel the force of the red sun fading in the distance. And he was incredibly hungry.

"Where are you going? Don't you want food?" Woof asked, trying to lure Gizzy into the cave.

Gizzy really felt it wasn't safe. "I think I'm just going to find my own food, but thanks anyway. I do appreciate the offer."

"But this is *yours*! You scared the little flig into the cave, and I handled the rest. You did the leg work. The hard work. Come on, we already agreed on how hungry you are. And how do you expect to sprout any whiskers if you're not getting any food in that belly of yours? Besides, I can hear your stomach growling from all the way over here!"

Woof's voice had started to get strangely deeper. Something wasn't right. As the sun continued its rapid descent and the foggy green of the moon began to take over, Woof started to act more peculiar.

"It's fine. I um, needed to go anyway," Gizzy said.

As Gizzy prepared to take off, Woof dropped to the ground in pain. He screamed and covered his face. As the sun dropped below the shelter of the blue trees and was entirely replaced by the bright-green moon, Woof began to transform. Coarse brown hair sprouted all over his body, and his clothes ripped off, slid to the ground, and disappeared as Woof's entire body started to grow bigger. Suddenly sharp white claws grew from his hands, then his hands morphed into giant paws. Part of Gizzy wanted to reach out and help, but the other part told him to run his butt off! He found himself rooted to the spot, petrified of what was happening but unable to make a decision. What kind of world was this?

When the moon reached its highest, brightest point in the night sky...the creature stood strong on all fours in his full reincarnation...Woof...was a transwolf!

Woof howled at the moon in a deafening and terrifying way. Squiggly and feathery and slimy creatures jumped up, took off, or flew out of the blue trees frightened by the howl...but it wasn't any ordinary howl or some kind of welcoming call...this was a battle cry!

Gizzy saw multiple glowing red eyes shimmer in the darkness of the cave. Woof wasn't alone! Not one, not two, but four more wolves jumped out of the cave and surrounded Gizzy, ready to pounce.

Woof was the biggest of the pack, clearly the alpha. The two wolves that moved behind Gizzy were gray and looked as though they might be brothers. The wolf to Gizzy's right was completely black with a red collar around his neck, as if he was owned, while the other wolves seemed stray. He could have been new to the pack, and Gizzy figured maybe he had to earn his right not to wear the collar. He also happened to be the smallest of the lot, and Gizzy figured he was probably bullied by the others.

The wolf to Gizzy's left was a bright golden blond with green eyes. A beautiful creature and the most fascinating of the pack. There was a symbol on the side of his left leg that appeared to be a magnifying glass. Interesting. Why would this wolf have a marking on his leg when the others showed no signs of markings?

"Grrrr! My brothers, enjoy the feast!" Woof said, then he let out another menacing growl.

The pack started to close in on Gizzy. Was this going to be the end? Was this really how Gizzy would go? In an altered world eaten by a pack of wolves? Gizzy closed his eyes and began to pray, and he was reminded of all the times he had asked for courage and strength and the ability to look after his sick mother. He suddenly remembered a time as a kid when his mother had forced him to go to church, and he had looked around at all the down-turned faces throughout the pews, wondering what it really meant to pray. But now he thought he understood it better. It was about nothing more than hope. And so he prayed for hope. One last chance to escape, to live. And if he wasn't allowed to live, Gizzy hoped to the god or gods of Altered that his mother would make a full recovery if he wasn't able to get back to her.

"Stop!" A booming voice called out of nowhere.

Gizzy immediately recognized the voice. It was the Air Guardian, Voice!

"Go back to the caves, you beasts! And you had better do it and do it now. If not, you know what the consequences will be!"

The wolves whimpered, gave Gizzy one last long stare, and headed back into the cave.

Gizzy sighed with great relief. His heart was beating so wildly, and he was sweating like crazy. His mind was still racing. Oh, goodness, how thankful he was to still be alive.

"Grrrrr, not like this!" Woof turned back, angered by the echoing voice. He jumped on top of Gizzy, refusing to be defeated by the Air Guardian. Woof was very heavy on top of Gizzy and pinned him down so he was unable to budge. Gizzy could smell Woof's horrid breath and the stink of his fur. Gizzy closed his eyes in fear, then realized that he must face the beast and fight for his life. He couldn't just give up now. He squirmed and squirmed under the weight of the beast and tried to break free, but it was no use. The wolf was too heavy and powerful, and Gizzy was in pain. He opened his eyes and looked deep into the eyes of the drooling wolf. Woof's dark brown eyes gazed back, and for a moment Gizzy could see the being inside the wolf, the entity who had promised to feed Gizzy and spare him of his hunger. But the being trapped inside was scared, and it was clear that the being never asked for this life; he was forced into it. Gizzy looked deeper into Woof's eyes and could see vast amounts of fear and sorrow within the being who was trapped inside and wanted out. But the beast was far too strong and took over and didn't let go. He was hungry for Gizzy.

"You don't have to do this," Gizzy said, begging to the being inside the beast, and Woof hesitated. The claws on the wolf grew longer. It looked like the being was fighting his way back, but the wolf was far too strong, and he reared back in anger and came down hard on Gizzy. There was so much confusion and adrenaline flowing that though Gizzy could feel the force of the blow, he couldn't feel the pain as intensely as he had anticipated; he only had a sensation of vibration and tingling throughout his whole body.

Woof put his face up to Gizzy's, baring his sharp and ugly teeth, drool hanging down from his angled jaw. "Now it's time to die," Woof said, and then he reared back and was about to pounce again when suddenly a bright light shot down from the sky. Voice! The pure-white beam shone on Woof and terrified him so much that he quickly jumped off of Gizzy and backed toward the cave. When he got inside

31

the cave, his red eyes went out, and there was only darkness again.

Everything was quiet, still, almost peaceful.

Transwolves, when in wolf form, were deathly afraid of the light.

Gizzy was still lying on the ground, his body pumping from the adrenaline. Knowing that Voice was nearby to protect him, he closed his eyes for a moment to bask in the peaceful night; he truly needed a rest!

Woof staggered down into the dark and eerie cave. He felt utter disgust when he looked at his four companions lazily lying around. He was so enraged by their failure to capture and kill the fresh human meat that he incited a pack fight. The wolves attacked one another, clawing and biting until fur was flying and blood was dripping. Then Woof felt satisfied that they had all been punished.

"Enough!" Woof howled to his pack.

The wolves stopped the melee and turned to face their master.

"At least we still have food for the night. You're lucky of that, my so-called friends."

The wolves looked at the slaughtered pig that Gizzy had chased into the cave. The corpse of the pig had started to rot, not that the wolves cared.

"Go. Eat. But next time we finish the job when we have the chance. Understood?"

The four wolves licked their chops. When Woof nodded, they rushed over to the slaughtered pig and tore it to scraps. Woof walked up the path toward the mouth of the cave and looked out, disappointed. He could see Gizzy lying on the ground, looking helpless.

The shy golden blond wolf with the magnifying glass marking walked up behind Woof and patted him with his paw to get his attention.

"What do you want!?"

"Master, I know that boy."

"Don't worry, we'll meet him again. I can promise you that."

Woof turned and walked away into the depths of the cave. The golden blond wolf followed him, and they joined in on the feast of the dead pig.

"Are you all right, Gizzy?" Voice asked.

Gizzy opened his eyes. Had he fallen asleep for a moment? He had thought he had heard faint voices in the distance. He looked around in the darkness, and it seemed safe enough. He found the strength and courage to stand and got to his feet, still surprised to be breathing and alive.

"Gizzy, are you OK?"

"Yeah, yeah. I'm OK, just give me a minute, please. That...that was the most terrifying thing I've ever...uh...I mean, thanks, Voice. I wouldn't be alive if it weren't for you."

"Unfortunately, on this planet there are far greater threats than transwolves, and I'm afraid you will have to face many of them, sooner or later. But for now, come along; you can't be out here in the dark for much longer. Let's take you back to the shack."

"Hey, wait! Where were you today?" Gizzy felt a touch of anger rising in his voice. "I waited for you all day!" Suddenly there was a painful throbbing in his body, but Gizzy tried to ignore it. Luckily the adrenaline was still flowing, though it was clearly starting to die down. Either way, Gizzy tried his best to ignore the pain. If there were more evil obstacles in this world, he'd have to learn how to grow tougher. "You know, I just got attacked by a pack of wolves, and now that I think of it, that wouldn't have happened if you'd kept your promise!"

"Gizzy...something's very wrong with you," Voice said, clearly worried. "Show me your right arm. Take off your jacket! Your sleeve is torn!"

Gizzy pulled his right arm out of his torn jacket sleeve to reveal a large gash. It was bleeding a lot, and the cut was fairly deep from the penetration of Woof's sharp claws. Gizzy was lucky the wound hadn't been worse. Looking at the open gash and dripping blood caused Gizzy to be even more aware of the pain and the fact that his body had been compromised. And he could suddenly feel something foreign inside him running in his blood, liked he had been given a sinister injection.

"Gizzy...you've been deeply cut."

"I'm having trouble thinking straight. Maybe I can find a simple way to patch it up. Yeah. I'm sure I could probably do that. I think…maybe…"

"You don't understand, Gizzy! You have to do more than just patch up the wound. If you don't find the cure for the wound, you'll turn into a transwolf!"

The words echoed in Gizzy's mind as he tried to think of a way to stop the bleeding, but he was too lightheaded now. Voice recognized Gizzy's scattered and frightened thoughts and instructed him to walk as far away from the cave as possible. Then he navigated Gizzy toward the clearing that led to the shack. From there, Voice had Gizzy scour the outskirts of the jungle until he found a deep-green algae-moss called spirudulse. It grew in triangular stacks among tall yellow reeds. Voice instructed him to pull off a strip of the thin top layer and wrap it around his bleeding arm, securing the wound. The spirudulse brought an instant cool and calm to the gash, and soon the throbbing slowed dramatically.

"Keep your arm wrapped until the morning, and it should be nearly healed by then. You have until the next sunset to find the cure. But you must hurry; you have very little time."

The Earth Kingdom was a dilapidated castle nestled among four snowcapped mountains. Its roof was covered in thick snow, and it only had one remaining stained-glass window that was encapsulated in ice. The Earth Kingdom was severely isolated, which kept almost everyone from finding the castle, which had been built for the Earth Guardian and his guests. Nobody else.

Ratchet, the Earth Guardian, was inside the castle, sitting by the high orange flames of a roaring fire. He was very unhappy that Voice was helping Gizzy to the Prophecy.

What good would that bring to their world? Wasn't there another way to return the boy to his own planet? Ratchet sensed that something wasn't right, and he feared that if Gizzy made it to the Prophecy, the entire world of Altered might be at risk, including Ratchet's dominion over the Earth Kingdom.

Witch had been the original occupant of the Earth Kingdom and the first-ever Earth Guardian. But the role was passed on to his second in command, Ratchet, when Witch was dethroned for violations of the Code of the Guardians.

Ratchet had been Witch's servant long before Witch became a guardian. Ratchet served Witch well and demonstrated great loyalty, courage, strength, and heart throughout Witch's tenure, even serving as Witch's subject when he needed to test out his new voodoo potions and spells. Witch was known as a Power-Born and carried the blood of those who held diverse and sacred supernatural abilities. Ratchet, ever the loyal servant, had spent hours frozen into a solid block of ice after Witch gyrated his hands and called out the Castamanorum spell, or the freezing spell. Witch's voodoo skills were in their infancy back then, and sometimes he had trouble releasing Ratchet from a spell or released him too early, like the time he was messing around with the Donum-Donum Barley levitation spell. Witch had been able to get Ratchet off the ground, then released the spell too quickly, and Ratchet fell hard on his head. They later joked that this was where Ratchet lost most of his brain cells.

In a sense, Ratchet owed his life to Witch, because Witch risked his own hide to save Ratchet when his Green Blood species was almost wiped out by the dreaded Bowsmen. At present, 95 percent of the Green Bloods were dead. Eradicated. Extinguished. The others had hidden away or vanished. Ratchet had gotten lucky, and after Witch had saved him from the certain death of bullets and singing arrows, Ratchet agreed to serve him until the very end.

The other Green Bloods all looked very similar to Ratchet with pale red skin, fully black eyes, and shocks of white hair. They had always been a rare species to Altered, but in the more recent passages of time, their hides had become truly valued by the villages of warm regions who used their strong and stretchy skin to make longboats and roofs and fine carpets. One day the Bowsmen discovered the hidden city of Grebliblian, which was nestled deep within a treacherous swamp. Witch happened to be nearby, plunging his hands into the sludgy swamp waters searching for rare fungi and nubeadle roots to increase the strength of his spells. He heard the awful sounds of the massacre and ran in that direction. Soon he came upon a frightened and shivering Ratchet, who was fleeing for his life. A Bowsman hunter appeared and aimed his long-iron shotgun at Ratchet, telling Witch to move, or else. Witch looked at the terrified Green Blood and felt deep, deep sympathy. He quickly turned to the Bowsman and cast a knobitic spell on the hunter, causing a wrenching pain in his gut and sending him to his knees, the long-iron shotgun falling from his hands to the ground.

When Witch was dethroned and the guardian role was passed onto Ratchet, Witch felt a sense of unease and uncertainty in Altered. Without his positon of power and might, he had lost his identity and struggled for a long time. Ratchet started to gain his own strength and power, and Witch felt unneeded, unnecessary, obsolete. One day, without a single word to Ratchet, Witch vanished, leaving Ratchet alone in the Earth Kingdom, feeling cold and abandoned.

"He can't go to the Prophecy! If he goes, I have an awful feeling the world will be destroyed! Voice says he knows what he's doing, but I just don't trust it! I can't! How could I? My instincts are telling me to stop the boy! That it's all too risky! As a guardian, isn't my highest duty is to protect Altered and everything held within? I can't sit back and watch this happen. But Voice is all over me about this whole thing, and I think he's monitoring my every move. There's only one choice now, and you, my friend, must stop the boy while I watch from afar. What do you say?"

Ratchet turned to face the person who was standing near the fire. His new partner-in-crime had brown spiky hair and a long face, tan skin, and a pirate suit that had been torn apart by the blazing winds of a cyclone. This boy was not from Altered, and Ratchet felt he could use him against Gizzy to save the planet.

"Yes, Master." The beat-up pirate accepted Ratchet's offer with a grin. This pirate knew Gizzy better than anyone. This pirate...was Clayton. However, it wasn't the boy Gizzy had known since kindergarten or even the best friend he had to leave behind after he had turned to a more sinister life back in Houston. Clayton's eyes were darker now than they had ever been, and he had a wild look about him. Coming to Altered had clearly changed Clayton and erased Cib forever, an incarnation of Clayton that had died the second he entered the whirling cyclone.

Ratchet had followed Voice's instructions at the shack and found Clayton floating near the Julipean beachhead and could see he needed urgent care. He had been bitten, and Ratchet assumed it was probably by one of those damn bludder sharks. Ratchet had taken Clayton in, fed him, bathed him, cleaned his wounds, and comforted him at the

Earth Kingdom. But no matter how many times he had tried to heal him, Ratchet could tell that something was very wrong with Clayton, like a mechanism had short-circuited in his brain, and he would be forever broken.

Ratchet, thinking of saving the planet, decided to use the now-deranged pirate to his advantage and persuaded Clayton that Gizzy had caused the cyclone and was the reason Clayton was now broken and stuck in Altered. If they let Gizzy make it to the Prophecy, he was convinced that Gizzy would destroy the world and kill everyone within.

Clayton had a fondness for his savior, and he and Ratchet had grown very close in a short period of time. It felt as if they were destined to be friends, even if they came from separate planets. Clayton had accepted Altered as his new home and would destroy anyone or anything that tried to disrupt his newfound life here. And now he was certain that Gizzy, his old friend and new nemesis, had to be stopped at any cost.

Chapter Three

The Curse Of The Bite

The following day, after another restless night on the floor on top of the alpaca blanket, Gizzy woke up. He didn't know how long he'd been asleep. He got up off the floor, yawned, and looked out the window. He noticed that the sun was hovering high overhead and looked like it was glowing in a weak way. Could it already be only a few hours until sunset? Gizzy was well aware now that the days on this planet didn't last long compared to the ones on Earth.

Gizzy turned from the window and spotted the hard-nettle bowl with the food inside. He was so tired that he had forgotten that Voice had helped him find an assortment of fruit covered in beeswax and slices of spongy yellow roots. Gizzy had been too exhausted to eat the night before, and now he reached inside the bowl and gobbled up the food too fast. His stomach quickly expanded and made him pay for it. Gizzy also felt fortunate that Voice had shown him where to find plant sleeves filled with fresh water. There were several full sleeves left over from the night before, but Gizzy couldn't manage to ration them, either. After drinking all of them, he sat down on the floor and stared at the bed he had quickly pushed against the door the night before. At least he felt much more energized this morning and was safe and sound, even though his arm was still in some pain.

His wounded arm! He had forgotten about that, too!

He unwound the spirudulse bandage and was shocked at the results. He shook his head, which sent his dreadlocks swaying, and took another look at his nearly healed arm. The skin had tightened the wound into a thin, pink line, and he could almost feel a natural static there. It was miraculous! Unfortunately, Gizzy could also still feel the curse of the transwolf pumping though his veins, and according to Voice, if he couldn't find a cure in a few short hours, he would become a transwolf.

Gizzy put on his gray jacket and moved the bed from blocking the door. Then he picked up the plant sleeves and tried to squeeze a few remaining drops of water out of them. Then he went outside and tossed the empty plant-water sleeves onto the ground. Ah, mornings in Altered. Where were those purple flute-like birds he had seen the other day? He sort of missed their pretty morning song. Then again, it could have been late afternoon, for all he knew. How did their song go again? Ah, he couldn't think straight with the red sun beating down so hot.

"I was wondering when you'd wake up. You're missing daylight!" Voice boomed.

"Whoa!" Gizzy said, frightened. "Man, sometimes you just come out of nowhere. And why didn't you just wake me!?"

"I tried!" Voice said. "You passed out last night. I couldn't wake you up, no matter how loud I screamed. Not to mention, and in case you've somehow forgotten, I'm just a voice!"

Gizzy really felt Voice was to blame for his current predicament. Couldn't Voice have just intervened earlier during Woof's attack? But if Gizzy really thought about it, if he had never gotten on the cruise ship in the first place, he wouldn't have gotten into this mess and would be back on

41

his own planet taking care of his mother. Even if she had a bad temper and treated him poorly, Gizzy knew there was good deep within her. His father's leaving all those years ago had instigated everything and turned his mother into an empty shell. And, who knows, maybe this crazy adventure would somehow lead him down a good path or toward some kind of solution to ultimately save his mother and put her back on the road of health and happiness.

"Gizzy. Gizzy!" Voice said, startling Gizzy from his thoughts.

"Yeah. So how do I find this cure?"

"You must head to Cobblebury, a small village west of here. Once there, you need to find an enchanted book called *To Summon or Not to Summon…Not to Be Confused with Salmon*. It will summon a fairy, and the fairy should be able to cure the curse and reverse the process streaming through your blood."

"A *fairy*?" Gizzy laughed. "How would a fairy be able to save me? That makes no sense!"

"Just trust me! Get to Cobblebury as soon as you can. They have a library that holds the enchanted book." Voice was getting agitated with Gizzy. "Remember, head west. It's a good distance, but you should be able to get there in time, if you're quick! I have matters of my own to deal with, otherwise I'd escort you."

"You're making me go alone?"

"I have some *very* important matters to deal with. It's personal. I'll find you before the day ends. Good luck, young Gizzy."

"Wait! Voice! Voice!"

Darn it. Voice had taken off again.

Gizzy faced to the west and started running across the clearing, then into the strangely quiet jungle, where he dodged waving vines and spikey shrubs.

A while later, he exited the shaded jungle and emerged into a very odd field. Orange-stemmed crops grew in circular patterns around the field, leaving the middle space wide open, almost like a small arena. Gizzy slowly walked through the empty space and tried to catch his breath. It was good to get a rest after so much running. The field was so peaceful, and he wondered when the last time was that he felt so calm and protected while in Altered. Had he seen such a vast and open space on dry land since he had arrived? He was happy to not have to run through the dark jungle anymore with its weirdo leaping creatures and treacherous vegetation. Though he badly wanted to, Gizzy realized he couldn't stay in the field and admire the landscape and take in the cool air. Time was not on his side. It was the last thing he had.

Suddenly, a flock of flying pigs sailed overhead, their beautiful black wings beating a mild song. The pigs seemed jolly as they glided over the field, up and up and soon out of sight. He needed to take this as a good sign and downplay his wounded arm and lack of time. Maybe this was the planet telling him that he would indeed find the book, summon the fairy, and save himself from becoming a hideous transwolf! Yuck!

Positive thoughts, Gizzy…positive thoughts.

Inside the Earth Kingdom, Ratchet was orchestrating his plan to stop Gizzy from getting to the Prophecy. He was happy to have Clayton in on the plan, but he couldn't trust that he would be successful in completing the task. Ratchet wasn't one to take that kind of risk, and he always seemed to have a Plan B.

Ratchet sat thinking about his duties as the Earth Guardian. It sometimes still struck him as odd that Witch had disappeared and Ratchet was now the sole protector of the land and everything within it. He and Voice were meant to balance each other out, Ratchet protecting the grounds and Voice protecting the air, but they were somewhat at odds now, and Ratchet continually weighed whether or not he could fully trust the Air Guardian.

Letvia, the Water Guardian, seemed to be a good and pure being. She protected the waters of the earth and all of the inhabitants within. Her counterpart was Inferno, the Fire Guardian. He was responsible for the fire, lava, and heat. Without a guardian, the elements would falter, fail, and create a great imbalance within the planet. Without an Earth Guardian, the ground would collapse. Without an Air Guardian, the atmosphere would create massive wind storms, erode the earth, and whip up the sea. Without the Water Guardian, oceans would overflow and spill over the land. And without the Fire Guardian, volcanos would erupt and the core of the planet would rise in temperature, burning the planet to a bleeding crisp from the inside. So if one guardian fell, the fate of the planet would be at utter risk and a replacement would need to be found on an incredibly urgent basis.

Many years ago, though, the situation in Altered looked very different. There was a single ruler, a king known as Alpha. Sadly, he was killed during a violent battle when the beings of Altered were warring against the Berserkers from the Flamanine world. When King Alpha died, his powers divided into the four elements and shot out of his body in spectacular lights of white, green, blue, and red, and those elements were absorbed by the four closest people to King Alpha at the time of his death. Voice absorbed the white air element, Witch absorbed the green earth element, Elizabeth absorbed the blue water element, and Barath absorbed the red fire element.

It was a hard transition for the four of them to instantly wield so much power and hold dominion over their elements. Everything was fine for a while, but soon Barath got carried away with his power and was unable to keep the fire element from taking control of him. Anger and rage built up inside him, and Barath became very selfish and isolated.

One day, Barath was in a particularly foul mood. He had been unable to quell the dark power of the fire, and Elizabeth had confronted him and tried to offer help. Barath resented the implication that the fire element was controlling him, and in a fit of rage, he shot a fireball at Elizabeth. Elizabeth was fast to react and shielded herself in an ever-revolving waterfall, but the sheer strength and harshness of the fire was able to eat through the water element and burned Elizabeth alive.

Witch and Voice were emotionally devastated and forced to act quickly. They couldn't risk allowing Barath to continue to wield the power of the fire element, and there was a slight vengeful taste in their mouths at the loss of the gentle Elizabeth. The two hastily chose execution as the only fitting punishment, and with unanimous agreement, they lured Barath to a meeting at Cloud Temple, read aloud his charge of murder, and sentenced him to death. Witch produced the Demonnuh-Axion curse from his book of voodoo and took Barath's life in an instant.

With two elements gone, Witch and Voice quickly asked Letvia to take her sister's place as the Water Guardian because it felt like the natural and honorable choice, then Voice asked the current Champion of Hell, Inferno, to be the Fire Guardian because Voice was certain that he, of all beasts, would be able to handle the heat of the element and find balance within its burning chaos.

Altered was made up of two dimensions—Overworld and Hell. Overworld was the land known as Altered, with diverse life, the dark-red sun, the expansive ocean, the beauty, the sprawling habitats. Hell was the second dimension, ruled by scorching lava, agony, vicious monsters, and ugly death. When someone or something died in Altered, they went to After-Life.

After Witch earned his new role as Earth Guardian, he got careless and spent most of his time working on spells instead of closely watching over the earth element. One day he was playing around with his spells, and Voice told him he ought to concentrate more on his duties and less on messing around. There were a lot more layers to the friction and tension between Witch and Voice, but this insult was the final straw for Witch and sent him over the edge. Witch balled up all his anger and threw the Conscial Removal spell at Voice, which caused him to lose his body but remain in existence as a voice that wandered through the air. According to the laws of Altered, an act against the ruler (with King Alpha dead, this meant any of the guardians) was considered high treason, so Voice, Letvia, and Inferno agreed to summon Witch to Cloud Temple, where he was unceremoniously stripped of his powers. The three guardians knew that a choice must be made quickly in order to retain the balance of the planet, making the inexperienced Ratchet, (Witch's right-hand man at the time), the quick and obvious choice.

***

Back inside the Earth Kingdom, Ratchet sat in his great armchair in front of the roasting fire. His magnificently glowing ballroom was enormous, and though it was beautiful, Ratchet felt alone…but then he sensed a presence.

"I know you're there, Voice. You should know better than to try to sneak up on me. As a guardian I know when another guardian is nearby. Tisk, tisk."

Voice had come to try to reason with Ratchet about helping Gizzy to the Prophecy. It was clear they had very opposing views about the matter, even if Ratchet didn't know what Voice's true intentions were.

"I need you to help Gizzy make it to the Prophecy. It has been two days, and he's already cursed by a transwolf. He can't possibly make it on his own. The boy just wants to go home. The more the guardians help him to the Prophecy the better chance he'll have of fulfilling his wish to return. Why do you want to deny him that?"

"I will never help anyone lead a threat to the Prophecy. This Gizzy is a foreigner to our world, and you of all people should know that we need to be careful if we want to protect our planet. Just let him become a transwolf and be done with it!"

"Look, he's not an idiot! He just has no idea what he's doing in our strange world, and do you really think someone who wound up here by accident and just wants to get home would be able to destroy Altered? He can't even catch or grow his own food! Regardless of your stance, I'm helping him."

"Well, I didn't want it to come to this, but you've really left me no other choice. Voice...I know where your body is!"

Ratchet's words haunted Voice and teased him with the thought that he might one day be reunited with his body after Witch had taken it from him. Oh, what a dream that would be. To feel the wind on his cheeks, the cool water on his skin, the rain pouring down, the warm heat of a gentle, crackling fire, the touch of another being.

"You better tell me where!" Voice's vocal presence boomed throughout the kingdom, echoing around the stone castle. It was powerful enough to knock out the fire in the fireplace, leaving behind a black, smoking ash.

"Now, now...don't be so impatient. You know what I want." Ratchet sneered, knowing that Voice was smart enough to anticipate the terms of the potential bargain. "If you help me get Gizzy to my Earth Kingdom, then I can capture him and protect the planet. If you complete your task, then I'll give you the coordinates to your body. If you oppose this deal, I swear I'll *destroy* your body, dance on the pieces, and feed them to the humubula beasts in the desert! Now, help me stop Gizzy, and I'll gladly give you the coordinates."

"You...you evil demon..." Voice had to pause and take a breath to calm himself. "How did you find my body in the first place?" Voice was now incredibly torn between helping Gizzy to the Prophecy and finally getting his body back.

"I was nearby when you lost your body. Have you forgotten how close I was with Witch? I was beside him for everything, even this…tragic event. And while it might not have been a fair thing to do, taking away your body, maybe you shouldn't have been so pushy and judgmental toward a guardian who risked his own life to save a nobody Green Blood who was hunted and deathly afraid. And anyway, don't pretend you're angry with me, Voice. It's Witch you want to get revenge on, not me. I was merely his confidant at the time, and now I'm offering you a fair deal, so choose wisely."

Meanwhile, time had passed quickly, and still Gizzy had found no sign of Cobblebury. He felt lost and realized sunset was fast approaching. It was as if the time of the sun dropping was unpredictable in this world by the standards of the time he knew back home; you just had to feel it here. He had been in Altered for two days now and had nothing to show for it except an often-empty stomach, a dry throat, and a curse that would more than likely turn him into a freakin' transwolf!

Gizzy could feel the curse within his bloodstream, the darkness taking over. Was it only a matter of time now? Suddenly, Gizzy looked up and spotted smoke swirling in the distance. Was that? It was! The village! Gizzy sprinted as fast as he could toward the rising smoke.

When Gizzy arrived at the village entrance, he found an unmanned guard tower.

"Hello?" Gizzy called up to the tower. No answer.

Gizzy walked through the raised gate and out into the middle of the village, which was still quite busy, considering it seemed to be moving toward evening. The dirt streets were occupied with what Gizzy could only consider strange-looking human types, with pale brown skin, short arms, and basically all the same physical characteristics, though the females had noticeable breasts hidden under their clothing. But each of them had equally large noses, big eyes, and none of them had any hair! Even the women were bald.

Everybody was staring at him, too, a bit confused by the different-looking stranger wandering through their town, though their stares didn't seem judgmental, only curious, and they didn't last long.

Seven small Victorian cottages lined Cobblebury. They were made of gray stone with brown-tiled roofs and narrow paths along the sides that carried water in and out. Triangular wells sprouted from the ground, and laundry hung on lines in the back of the cottages. There was a giant house near the end of the main road, and Gizzy assumed it was where everybody lived, as the other cottages seemed to be places of business. Or maybe they doubled as businesses and homes? Gizzy wasn't sure. But there were crops all along the road and along the cottages and up on the hills, and it seemed as if the whole town was growing food to feed the entire community.

Gizzy looked around as he walked. There was a blacksmith, a bakery, a clothing store, a hospital, a schoolhouse, and the Cobblebury library. It really felt like a pleasant community. If only Earth was more like this village. Maybe it was some kind of Utopia?

Gizzy called out, "Hello? I'm looking for an enchanted book!" But nobody responded, though a few smiled and seemed to want to say something.

Suddenly, there was a crash of pots and pans from the bakery. With little sunlight remaining, Gizzy sped off toward the crash. When he arrived, he saw a boy on the floor of the bakery, surrounded by pots and pans. Oddly, the boy looked a lot like Gizzy and pretty much nothing like the others in the village. He had short brown hair, was quite muscular, and was wearing a skinny T-shirt. He had a giant belt around his waist with the letter B on it and carried a small yellow backpack. The pack looked really rough, like it had taken a pounding for years. Gizzy wondered if the bag was special to the boy and whether or not he carried it around for sentimental reasons, rather than practical.

"Are you OK?" Gizzy asked the boy. He reached out his hand and pulled the boy up.

"Thanks. Yeah, I'm OK."

Gizzy was surprised at how much the teenage boy looked like a human.

"Well, I'm Brayden," the boy said. Then he took on a surprised look. "Wow. I never see anyone who looks anything like me, but you kinda do."

They eyed each other suspiciously. Then Gizzy said, "Yeah, I was thinking the same thing. That's pretty odd."

"Well, you're clearly not from around here. And you're not an NPC, either. And doubtful you're a Justment."

"Um...what are those?"

"You know. Look around. NPCs. Only Nose People Characters live in Cobblebury. Well, until I moved here, I guess. Anyway, that was a few months back. And Justments are beings who…wait, so what are you doing here? Did you get lost? I only ask because nobody ever comes out to Cobblebury."

"Well, to start, my name's Gizzy, and I really need some help."

"Oh, OK. Help with what?"

"Well, it's nothing crazy. It's just that I've been…well…cursed."

"Cursed? Um, sure. Nothing crazy about that…" Brayden said, and started to walk away.

"Wait! Um…" Gizzy felt confused as he watched Brayden walking away. He quickly decided to go after him and jumped in front of Brayden. "Wait! I'm going to turn into a transwolf soon, and I need to find an enchanted book. Voice told me to come here."

"Voice…" Brayden hesitated with shock written all over his face. Voice, a name from the distant past that Brayden had forgotten. But now a remembrance was welling up inside him from deep in the back of his mind. A wave of nostalgia came over him. Suddenly, Brayden said, "Wait! An enchanted book? Do you mean…"

"It's called *To Summon or Not to Summon*. Do you know of it!?"

"I think I might know where that is! Come on, follow me!"

Brayden took off running. Gizzy chased after him down the street and up the steps of the old Cobblebury library. Brayden threw the front door open and jumped over the wooden bannister, ignoring the librarian who pulled her glasses down her big nose as she watched the rushing boys fly past her. When she realized it was Brayden, she sighed and continued sorting the books on the cart in front of her. Brayden had only been in the village a few months, and the Nose People Characters started to recognize the foreigner as a klutz and a bit of a screw-up. None of the townspeople held it against him, as the Nose People Characters were a very accepting race, but he had inadvertently caused a bit of trouble in town since he had arrived. Once he had accidentally tipped over the small wooden water tower on the hill overlooking town, and he was often looking at the ground or up at the sky thinking, which left him vulnerable to bumping into busy pedestrians.

Brayden darted between the stacks of the "Magic and More" section, then he abruptly stopped halfway down the stack. "Oh no! It's gone. I swear, it used to be here!" Brayden looked closely at the row of books. He pushed a few aside, then he turned to Gizzy.

"Are you sure? Maybe it was shelved somewhere else? Or we could ask the librarian." Gizzy really hoped it wasn't true. He had such little time left before he would turn into a transwolf. Gizzy frantically pushed books aside. Books of all shapes and sizes—triangles, squares, cubic books, circular books, hollow books, books made out of goo or tar or bark or fine grasses. He had never seen anything like it. Soon Brayden snapped out of it and joined in, and books were flying everywhere and falling to the floor, piling up to their ankles.

When there were no more books on the shelf where the enchanted book should have been, Brayden said, "I feel so terrible! You're following Voice's instructions, and I've...I've failed him."

Before Gizzy could respond, Brayden ran away from the stacks, jumped the bannister, and took off down the road. Gizzy ran to the checkout desk, but the librarian was gone. All that remained was her stack of books.

Gizzy ran after Brayden, following him as best as he could. Had Gizzy been running for days? It sure seemed like it, especially with his stomach growling again. He hoped it might forget how hungry he was.

Hunger. Wolves. Gizzy stopped and looked toward the green moon hanging overhead, its mellow waves flowing off its surface. Oh no. Gizzy ran again.

"We're too late," Brayden said, when Gizzy caught up to him. All the Nose People Characters had gathered in the big village home to sleep. Brayden knew that he needed to act fast if he was going to save himself and the town before Gizzy turned into a transwolf and made things too interesting for comfort.

"Brayden I—" Gizzy started, but before he could finish, he collapsed in agonizing pain, screaming out for help. Gizzy writhed around on the ground, turned on his side, and dug his heels into the dirt, spinning in circles.

Brayden thought quickly and grabbed Gizzy by the arm. He dragged Gizzy through the dirt with all his might and was able to kick open the secret door at the back of the clothing store and pull Gizzy inside. This was where Brayden was temporarily living, hidden from the locals in the shared main house. The room contained a small bed, some clothes draped over a thin line, and a red backpack hanging from a nail on the wall.

Gizzy looked up from the floor. This space was much cozier and neater than the shack he had been living in.

Gizzy attempted to get up off the floor, but another jolt of pain shot through him, and he started going through the same transformation as Woof had the night before. Convulsions, coughing, heavy pains in his chest, limbs, and neck. Gizzy tried to get up again, but he stumbled and fell back down.

Brayden scooted away from Gizzy and braced himself against the wall.

Gizzy tried to breathe and think positive thoughts, but rolling on the floor with his skin tingling and burning, all he could think of was how much he missed the familiarity of Earth and how badly he wanted to go home.

Soon, he would become a transwolf.

Chapter Four

The Canine

"I...I just...feel so angry," Gizzy said. He was on all fours, his body now covered in black fur. In no time he had morphed from a teenage boy into a terrifying wolf. Gizzy's voice was much rougher now, but he still had his blue eyes. He had sprouted razor-sharp claws and teeth that would frighten anyone...except Brayden wasn't scared at all. Instead he was fascinated by the transformation.

"Remarkable," Brayden said, still backed against the wall of his little room. He reached out toward Gizzy, as if checking whether this new wolf version of Gizzy was a friend or foe.

Gizzy was bewildered, full of anger and frustration at what he had become, confused about his new primal body, threatened by Brayden being there and having seen Gizzy at his most vulnerable. He questioned why he even felt this way, given that Brayden was possibly the closest thing he had to a peer or a friend at this point. Also, sadly, Brayden might be his best chance at survival. Even though Gizzy knew that Brayden wasn't a threat, he was confused as to why Brayden would want to help him and questioned his motives. Was he going to turn Gizzy in so he could be subjected to scientific experiments at the hands of the seemingly peaceful Nose People Characters? And who was Brayden, anyway? Why had he only been in Cobblebury a short time? Where had he come from? The thoughts rushed through Gizzy's head, making him dizzy, and suddenly he felt so threatened by Brayden's presence that he growled at him.

Brayden yanked his hand away and suddenly felt uncomfortable with his new guest, who was, after all, a sharp-toothed transwolf. Brayden made a run for the door, threw it open, and quickly locked it on his way out, leaving a bewildered Gizzy trapped inside.

Gizzy jumped at the door to try to break it open, but it was no use. Now that he had paws instead of hands, opening the door would be an…im-paws-ibility. Even though Gizzy was still conscious of the fact that he was a human deep inside the beast, he could feel the anger of the wolf rising inside him, causing an inner struggle. Would he eventually want to eat Nose People Characters and Justments and the other beautiful creatures of Altered just like the other wolves? Would he be so drawn to the wolf part of himself that he would join the wolf pack back at the cave?

Gizzy had been trapped inside the room all night and had spent those late hours contemplating how to cope with becoming a transwolf while trying to deny and push away his new wolf-like instincts. His sense of smell had become so sharp that he could pick up the scents of a variety of flowers halfway across the village. He could easily smell Brayden outside, so close and so intense. Was he savoring the smell? Was it attracting him? Was that saliva forming and a rumbling in his stomach? Gizzy shook his head to get rid of the thoughts and tried to throw off the instinct. Gizzy attempted to walk in circles, but he had trouble at first getting used to being on four legs; he stumbled and fell several times until he got somewhat used to the stance and the movement. It was also odd seeing things so low to the ground, only a few feet up compared to his teenage-boy height. Gizzy also had difficulties being covered in fur; it itched so darn much! Once he got used to being on four legs, Gizzy spent a good deal of the night walking circles around ı, rubbing his sides and shoulders against the ı all his itches.

ıours drifted by, Gizzy finally managed to tire d fall asleep, and the green, hazy moon eventually replaced the deep-red sun of Altered. The flupleswoops tweeted their morning song as they flew overhead, orange-and-gray rabbits came out from their burrows and boinged around town, and the villagers went quietly about their usual business of tending to their crops, looking after the laughing children, mailing letters written with invisible ink, hammering armor and weapons, and enjoying the early-morning breeze.

Brayden had spent the entire night guarding his little room from the outside. He woke from a very uncomfortable night of sleep in the dirt, propped against his door like a vagrant. He stood up, gave a big yawn, and peeped through the small window confirming just what he had suspected— Gizzy was still sleeping and had returned to his human state. Gizzy's clothes had disintegrated the night before when his transwolf transformation took place, and Brayden had already planned to offer some of his own clothes in the morning. But he was surprised to find that Gizzy's clothes had miraculously reanimated, and on all the right parts, too!

Brayden walked to a nearby orchard and broke off a thin branch holding several snap apples. The snap apples were yellow and the size of grapes. They tasted sour, but each one had the nutrient density of an entire meal of superfoods. When Brayden got back to his place, he carefully turned the lock on the door, opened it slowly, and entered the small space. The slight noise woke Gizzy, and he sprang to his feet, his eyes looking tired. His animal instincts hadn't quite left him, even though he was human again.

"Ah!" Brayden said, almost dropping the small snap apple branch.

"Oh. Sorry," Gizzy said. "You scared me. What are those?"

Brayden held out the little branch with several snap apples dangling. "Just take one. You'll feel better."

Gizzy plucked off one of the snap apples. "So…how do I eat it?"

"You just pop it in your mouth. They're sour, but you'll feel like you're stuffed after eating one."

Gizzy popped the little yellow ball in his mouth and immediately made a face. "Jeez, talk about sour."

"Told ya," Brayden said.

While Gizzy finished eating the tiny apple, Brayden packed the rest into the red backpack and gave it to Gizzy. "Here, so you don't go hungry today."

"Thanks," Gizzy said. "I appreciate you being so kind, especially after…hey, so what exactly happened last night? Was that all…real?"

"You mean you writhing on the floor; sprouting gross wolf hair, fangs, and claws; and generally turning into a psycho wolf? Check, check, and check."

"Brayden, I'm really sorry about that, but it's not something I can control. I don't even really remember any of last night. It's all so foggy. I was clawed and infected by a transwolf in the jungle the other night. Here, look." Gizzy pulled his arm out of his torn jacket sleeve to show Brayden the wound.

"There's barely a trace of a scar there," Brayden said, pointing.

Gizzy looked down in amazement; his arm had nearly healed already. "Dang, that spirudulse works fast!" Gizzy slipped his arm back into the jacket and zipped it three quarters.

"So, what now?" Brayden asked.

"Thank you for everything you've done for me, but I really need to get going."

"Already? But I still need answers! You're the only living thing I've seen that looks anything like me and you wander into the village looking for some magical book and randomly turn into a wolf at night. And on top of that you know who Voice is! And now you're telling me you need to get going?" Brayden stood in front of the doorway. He wanted answers and was determined not to let Gizzy leave without knowing what was going on.

"Like I said, I need to find that book to get rid of this curse. I told you I was attacked by a transwolf, and now I *am* a transwolf! You saw enough evidence of that last night, I'm sure. And I'm not even from this planet. My planet's called Earth, and I honestly just want to go home. Voice said that the only way I can get home is by getting to the Prophecy. I hate to be rude, but I really need to go and find that book!"

Brayden widened his stance at the door.

"Brayden, please move!"

"I have more questions."

"Oh no, look out behind you!" Gizzy said. "It's the Goodyear Blimp!"

Brayden stiffened up and quickly turned around. Gizzy took this opportunity to push Brayden aside and run out the door.

"Goodbye, and I'm really sorry!" Gizzy called over his shoulder as he ran away. Gizzy couldn't believe Brayden fell for that old trick, although it was only an old trick on Earth. Yeah, well, anyway. Gizzy didn't want to put Brayden in any more danger, and he had a lot of ground to cover in little time.

"Wait!" Brayden yelled, but he stumbled and fell as he tried to run out the door. Typical, clumsy Brayden. By then Gizzy had already disappeared past the rolling hills outside the village.

Brayden got up and dusted himself off. "Wait a minute…the Prophecy… Gizzy knows what the Prophecy is!?" Brayden ran as fast as he could over to the guard tower where two bulky guards were lurking inside. Though they were supposed to be posted at all hours of the day, they were notorious for ditching their duties and heading down to the pub for a pint or two of shimmy shime. The guards took off their shiny helmets when Brayden arrived.

"Guys! It's a miracle!"

"What is it now, Brayden?" The guards were very aware of Brayden's clumsy ways and had grown tired of him continually coming to bother them with minimal complaints.

"The Chosen One was here! He stayed in my room last night and said he wasn't from this planet. He also said he's going to the Prophecy, and you know what that means!" Brayden was incredibly excited, and as he blurted out this revelation, the guards became excited, too. Big smiles broke out on their harsh faces as they had been waiting for this day for so long.

"We must help this adventurer get to the Prophecy!" one of the guards said.

Brayden cheered with excitement, and the guards clinked their spears.

"Brayden, nobody can know about this, and that's on Tayren's orders. This Chosen One must have come to stop the guardians. Finally! Now, go and find him, and help bring him to the Rebellion. They'll know what to do with him. I'm giving you this task because…well…" he looked at the other guard, clearly not convinced of what he was about to say, "we believe in you."

Brayden's eyes lit up. He had never been trusted with anything since arriving in the village. The Nose People Characters had been very kind to Brayden and welcomed him into their lives, even if he was clumsy, often got in the way, asked too many questions, and they were overall just generally suspicious of him. But now it was time for Brayden to return the favor and redeem himself.

"Yes, sir! I will go and find Gizzy and take him to the Rebellion! If I leave now I should be able to catch up with him before he gets too far!"

Brayden ran off, and the guards put their helmets back on, returned to their posts, and stood strong with big smiles on their faces, hopeful for the future. What they didn't realize was that someone was lurking behind the guard tower. Clayton had been hiding there the entire time and had heard everything. He had been sent to the area on Ratchet's orders, who had felt the presence of Gizzy in the area.

"My god...so this little village is helping Gizzy get to the Prophecy!" Clayton opened up his backpack and searched around. His eyes blinked red, then yellow. Something was definitely infecting him. "My master told me to stop Gizzy from going to the Prophecy...and the Nose People Characters of this village are going to help Gizzy make it there..." Clayton pulled out a few metallic spheres from his backpack. Wires dangled from the spheres, and Clayton clipped the wires together, then placed a few spheres on the tower, where they suctioned against the wood. Then he pressed a shiny red button at the top of each sphere, and a timer popped up and began counting down from ten minutes. "Let's see if they'll be able to help him after this."

Just after Brayden darted after Gizzy, he passed the Cobblebury library and skidded in his tracks. He knew Gizzy would probably shun him again, so Brayden needed something to gain his trust and attention, a reason to get Gizzy talking with him again so he could lead him to the Rebellion.

Brayden rain into the library, jumped the banister again (to the chagrin of the librarian), and checked every aisle and shelf, until finally he found a note that had fallen onto the floor and landed under one of the stacks in the "Magic and More" section. Brayden picked up the note and unfolded it. The paper was fairly crisp. The note read:

Ha! I've taken the mythical book to learn a thing or two from it! If you want to find me and challenge me for the return of the mighty book, meet me at the Green Lageen! Love, Betsy the Troll X

PS: Pick me up a pint of shimmy sham if you have a minute before you come looking! Cheers.

"Dah, it was Betsy!" Brayden said, as he crumpled the note. Then he breathed heavily, uncrumpled the note, folded it, put it into his pocket, and ran out of the library to find Gizzy.

And not Gizzy nor Brayden nor the guards nor any of the Nose People Characters were aware of the ticking spheres being placed around town, their clocks winding closer and closer toward destruction.

Gizzy made it back to the shack. The quicksand pool behind the shack looked like it was bubbling, and it really freaked Gizzy out. He rammed his shoulder into the shack door, sending some frightened orange hobble frogs leaping thirty feet high over the treetops. Whoops. He didn't mean to be so aggressive about it, but he was incredibly winded and needed a minute to sit down so he could just breathe and think things over. Gizzy set the red backpack full of snap apples on the floor and made it over to the bed and took a seat. Had he stopped running or going from *A* to *B* to *C* since he had arrived on this crazy planet? Everything was happening so fast, and with such little daylight in Altered contrasted with the drawn-out night, it worried Gizzy that his future might be full of so much darkness, fear, and despair. But wasn't he a positive person? Wasn't Earth Gizzy bright and happy and glowing? Had being in Altered changed him, or had it just worn him out with all the running and tension and freaky creatures?

Gizzy lied down on the bed, and his mind continued to wander, deeper and deeper into the Altered world. OK, so he had definitely changed. He could feel it pulsing through his blood. The slash of the transwolf had gotten to him and infected his body and spirit. But Gizzy didn't want that to define him. He needed to find that book and figure out if there was a way to cure himself, even if he was now a day beyond the deadline Voice had given him. Maybe the fairy from the book could grant him leniency? Or maybe there was a special berry or a root or an herb or some kind of spell that could turn him back to a full teenage boy again? He had sure dreamed of an adventure, but he hadn't expected anything quite like this.

Suddenly he thought of his mother and the last time he had seen her before setting off on the cruise. He could see her clutching the other ticket in her hand, rolling around in the bed. She had been barely conscious from all the drinks she'd had that day. Had Gizzy really taken the cruise because he had wanted an adventure, or was he running from his mother? Had he abandoned her? The guilt of it all rose up in his throat, and he turned over in the bed and looked at the dirty floor of the shack, as if he might throw up the sadness.

It still pained Gizzy to think that he was capable of saying those cruel words to his mother, and he figured with the cyclone destroying the ship and sending it, presumably, to the bottom of the Gulf of Mexico, he was probably considered missing at best and dead at worst. And what would his mother think? Had she gotten the news in Houston? If so, was she devastated? Relieved? He didn't want to believe she would ever feel relief at the loss of him.

65

No, what a stupid thought, Gizzy! But hadn't she in a way deserted him when his father left with that stewardess from Dallas? Hadn't she hidden herself in a bottle of alcohol and a veil of tears since that day? And hadn't Gizzy been forced to grow up too quickly and lose a good portion of his young life, if not most of it, to taking care of her?

The thoughts were so overwhelming that Gizzy felt sharp pains in his head, and he jumped up and smashed the small wooden table. It broke into several pieces. Gizzy's hand hurt now. He clutched his fist and lied back down on the bed. Gizzy had a lot of trouble getting comfortable. He covered his head with his good hand and let the other one fall to his side. He was trying hard to forget about his mother, the missing magical book, and the fact that he was now a transwolf.

But, hey, he had to think on the bright side of things. Maybe being a transwolf wouldn't be so bad? Sure, he would be a dangerous animal at night that could harm anything within reach, but maybe he could learn how to control the beast within and not let it overtake him. Perhaps with the right training he could control the awesome powers of the transwolf and become a super hero! Gizzy started to like this thought. Most superheroes back on Earth had a questionable past, right? Batman, Daredevil, Spiderman...the list could go on! Having an alcoholic mother with a missing father was a fairly common character trait, too. And Gizzy now had the power of becoming a transwolf that could maybe do good for Altered. Super Dog! No. Wolf Man! No. The Canine! Getting better, Gizzy! He laughed at himself, trying to think positively about becoming the super hero that every creature or person needed.

By day: a lazy, no-good slob with no job who had to randomly win a cruise from a drawing to bring a small adventure into his life.

By night: The Canine! Hunting menacing creatures and defending those who needed it! He would be a good hero. Wait a second. Gizzy suddenly thought about how he had won the cruise ticket. He had never heard of anyone winning something as big as a cruise from a Teens for Teens raffle. Why hadn't he looked deeper into that? What were the odds of him winning? And why hadn't he recalled ever putting his name in for a drawing like that? Didn't kids often just win a free slice of pizza or a few games of cosmic bowling? He hadn't recognized the name of the cruise line, either, but he had figured maybe it was one of those cheapo brands, like those European airlines nobody has ever heard of that pack people in like sardines and charge twenty dollars a ticket.

Think, Gizzy. What was the name of that cruise line? Oblivia! That was it! Not the most intelligent or marketable name for a cruise company. So, wait. Oblivia. Could it have been fake? Could his landing on Altered have all been planned? Staged? A set-up? A fraud?

No! Impossible! Gizzy figured he must be turning paranoid. Maybe it was just a side effect of being The Canine. Nobody and nothing on Earth could control the weather and create a cyclone, and who could have predicted that pirates were going to randomly show up and hijack the ship? But, wait. Nothing on Earth could do that…but what about—

Brayden suddenly burst through the door and stopped in the doorway. He was dripping with sweat and had to bend over and put his hands on his knees. His chest was heaving in and out, and he sounded like a plump walrus.

"Jeez, you scared me half to death!" Gizzy said, now up and alert on the edge of the bed, ready to attack.

"Wait…just…wait," Brayden said, exhausted. He held up a finger, then put his hand back on his knee. When he had regained his breath a bit, he stood up and looked at Gizzy. "I'm here to help you! And…I found this!" Brayden held up the note. "I know where the book is!"

Gizzy grabbed the note and read it. "The Green Lageen?" Gizzy threw the note back at Brayden, and it hit his chest and landed on the floor. "Sounds like a budget spa in Iceland."

"Iceland?" Brayden was confused. He had never heard of Iceland before. "What's Iceland? Is it up by the Earth Kingdom?"

"No, never mind. It's not here on Altered. Forget it. Anyway, so where's the Green Lageen?"

Brayden pulled a compass from his tatty yellow backpack. "Here, check out my compass. Just put in the coordinates, and it'll point you to wherever you need to go! I already entered the coordinates for the Green Lageen!" Brayden handed the compass to Gizzy.

Gizzy turned the compass around, ran his fingers over the strangely soft casing. Then he picked up the red backpack of snap apples, put it on his back, nodded at Brayden, and walked out of the shack toward the jungle.

"Wait, am I coming with you or not?" Brayden asked.

Gizzy stopped and turned around. "No. I need to do this myself. I mean…what if I become The Canine again?"

"The Canine? What the heck is that?"

"You know, 'Grr, I'm a crazy transwolf who's going to eat you!' That kind of thing." Gizzy turned back to the compass and walked off, staring down at the dial.

Brayden stood in the doorway watching him go. Then he yelled, "Oh, come on, Gizzy! I need to know more about you! Can't you at least tell me *something*? Maybe something *deeper* you might want to confide?"

As Gizzy continued on toward the Green Lageen, he thought about what Voice had said about invoking the fairy to cure the curse. A fairy sidekick for The Canine? Hmm…he sure liked that idea!

Chapter Five

The Green Lageen

X 301, Y 64, Z 288. The numbers continued to run through Gizzy's head as he got ever closer to the Green Lageen. Even though he didn't know anything about this place or what he might encounter, Gizzy still found the courage to push forward. He knew there wasn't a lot of daylight left, and Gizzy wondered what would happen if he got to the location and turned into a wolf again. Would he attack every living thing in sight? Or would the inhabitants of this Green Lageen be even more ferocious and scary and have tentacles or sharp scales or shoot fire, attacking him first?

No. Gizzy needed to put these negative thoughts out of his head.

But what if this Betsy character who took the enchanted book that Gizzy desperately needed turned out to be some great big beast who could devour Gizzy in one gulp? Stop it, Gizzy!

The red backpack full of crab apples gently bounced against Gizzy's back as he walked on through a golden meadow in a seemingly peaceful area. Every time he got near a grouping of flowers, flutterflies would shoot into the air, leaving a trail of copper dust. Gizzy stopped and smiled. But he had to move on.

For whatever reason—the anticipation, the excitement, the fear—Gizzy started to run as he edged closer and closer to the coordinates. He had long left the beautiful golden field behind and now past through a smelly overrun swamp covered in black gnarled vines and mud and carcasses of dead creatures he wouldn't even have recognized if they were alive. This clearly wasn't the kind of place where a person would want to build a vacation home! The putrid smell invited hundreds of thumb-thick gray flies to the area; their fat wings buzzed as they hovered over the carcasses. Tiny creatures chewed on the skins and the meat of the dead beings, and Gizzy turned it up a notch and ran even faster through the murky mud and trenches until he finally managed to pass through and arrive into a dark open space.

Woo. Gizzy needed a minute to just breathe. He rested one hand on his quad and lifted the compass with the other. He was really, really close to his destination and still trying to get some of his wind back. His ears were rushing with the sound of waves, yet he still felt he could hear the disgusting creatures in the distance, snacking on the parts of the dead.

The ground around Gizzy was black and covered in little chips of wood. He had been too exhausted to notice before. If a person threw down a match here, the whole nature floor would go up in flames!

Gizzy looked up. The air around was smoky and cool, like everything was turning a light gray. Through the thin veil of grayness, he made out a small, decrepit building. He walked up to the structure and realized it was...well, a tavern. Really? An old-fashioned Irish pub stood in the middle of nowhere here in Altered. How odd. Most of the windows had been broken and were boarded up, and the door had so many dark scuffs that it had surely been repeatedly kicked by belligerent customers. Or maybe the swamp creatures out having a late-night frolic. The white-and-red brick walls were covered in purple vines and slick moss, indicating that it hadn't been looked after in many years. With this kind of derelict Irish pub, Gizzy could easily imagine the kind of patrons who would frequent this place.

Gizzy stepped up to the door and tried to turn the handle, but it was firmly locked. There was a sign on the door: "BASICALLY CLOSED." Gizzy laughed. Whatever that means? He stepped to a window and wiped away some of the dirt and grime to peek inside. He couldn't really make out much, so he spat on his hand and tried to wipe the window clean. Then he knocked hard to see what would happen.

Nothing.

Then he saw a sudden movement inside. Or was he imagining things? Night was coming on, and maybe it was just a transwolf delusion?

Then he heard a loud crash in the pub! Gizzy could feel the cold of night coming on, the darkness shifting, and if that was Betsy inside, Gizzy knew he really needed to get to him and grab the book before nightfall.

Gizzy kicked at the door. Hard. After several tough shots (like the door hadn't experienced this a few hundred times before) he was able to force his way in. When the door broke off its hinges and fell to the ground, Gizzy found himself inside the murky Green Lageen.

"Get out!" said a strange creature hiding behind the bar. "You get out of here right now, trespasser!"

"Are you Betsy?"

"Yes, Betsy. Now get out!"

"Is this your bar?" Gizzy slowly walked forward.

"It's not, but you should still get out! Leeeeave, trespasser!"

Gizzy stopped and smiled. "If it's not your bar, and you're in here digging around, doesn't that make you a trespasser, too?"

The rummaging behind the bar stopped. "Um. I found it first! What are you doing bothering me here?"

"You stole a book from the Cobblebury library and left a note."

"It was just a joke, you damn trespasser! I'm sorry!"

"Betsy?" Gizzy asked, walking closer to the bar. He used great caution as he approached. "It's OK, I'm not going to hurt you. I just really need that book."

"No!" Betsy jumped out from behind the bar. He was a small, fat troll with green skin, no hair, and no nose. He had stubby legs and struggled to run but was quick enough to get to the backroom, slam the door, and lock it behind him. Gizzy had been in such shock at the fat little troll that he didn't react much. He had noticed that Betsy was wearing a dark shoulder bag, and Gizzy assumed the book was inside. As Gizzy walked toward the backroom door, he noticed the slight beam of the remaining sun was no longer breaking through the gray mist outside. Gizzy's skin slightly tingled, and he knew it wouldn't be long before he transformed into The Canine again…

Gizzy felt a great sense of urgency now. He needed to get the book immediately and run as far away as possible from any living, breathing thing. Otherwise…

He sprinted up to the door and yelled, "Listen to me, Betsy! It's very important that I get that book!" Gizzy tried the door handle, but it wouldn't turn. He could hear Betsy's body scraping against the door; he was clearly leaning against it to stop Gizzy from entering.

"Something really bad is going to go down, and I need that book to stop it!"

"No! You can't have it! It's mine!" said Betsy with his foul crackly voice. "I left that note on an impulse. It was meant as a joke. I don't know what I was thinking. I'm a troll! What do you expect? In the future, I'll add menacing pictures to my notes. Anyway, if I can just figure out how to make the magic in this book work I can use it to my advantage!"

"What do you even want the book for, anyway? I actually *need* it!" Gizzy said.

No response. But Gizzy could hear Betsy breathing hard behind the door.

Gizzy looked around, trying to find another way in. He noticed an attic door above the bar. He climbed onto the bar top, knocking over a few old pint glasses covered in cobwebs. The glasses shattered on the floor.

"You're paying for that!" Betsy yelled.

"You don't even work here!" Gizzy yelled back, then he continued into the attic. The sun was basically gone now, and he didn't have much time left.

74

Once inside the attic, Gizzy could see nothing but cobwebs, although in the far corner he did notice a skeleton in a sitting position, as if one of the Nose People Characters had just died here waiting for a pint of brew. Gizzy walked over to the skeleton and saw a chain with an amulet hanging from the neck bones. "Allanin" was engraved on the amulet. Was it someone's name? A place? A word that had a different meaning? If it was a name, then something bad must have happened to Allanin and he got himself trapped up here…or maybe he was hiding from something. Gizzy ran his fingers over the chain, felt its coolness.

"It'll make me rich! People will pay good money for a book like this! It's what I do! I'm a thief, don't you know?" Betsy continued from down below.

Gizzy crawled through the small spaces and batted away the cobwebs, avoiding the red-and-black spiders everywhere until he was finally standing above the room where Betsy was hiding. Gizzy gathered his strength, breathed in deeply, and jumped up as high as he was able, bringing his knees to his chest. His hope was that the wood had been weakened over time, warped, maybe eaten from the inside by some kind of termite-like creature that belonged only to Altered. With all his strength he came down hard on the flooring and smashed through, sending him crashing down.

Dust blew up into the air. Smashed boards and nails and rivets were all over the floor in a pile of rubble. Gizzy's head was spinning. He blinked over and over, but he couldn't see straight. Sharp colors floated across his vision. He could somewhat make out the green troll, but everything was blurry. Gizzy tried to lift his head and get up, but he immediately fell down. He was only conscious for a few more seconds, then everything went black.

Gizzy was inside a cave. The cave was covered in a shiny yellow ore that encrusted the whole cavern. He felt so lost and transplanted. Where the heck was he? And how did he get here?

Gizzy noticed that his hands were strangely small, like those of a young child. He realized he was no longer inside his own body and must have been transported inside the body of a small child who was inside the cavern. The understanding came to him so abruptly that it felt like an information injection. So strange.

So…where was he in time? Or when was he?

Gizzy could hear whispering in the distance, and the child walked toward the sound. Gizzy was now certain that he was only an observer inside the child and had no control at all. It was fascinating and strange seeing everything through the eyes of the child. But it was also an awful, helpless feeling.

When the child finally stopped, Gizzy noticed they were high in the cavern, and the child looked down on three figures who were whispering among themselves. Gizzy figured they might be the Justment beings Brayden had mentioned in the village. Obviously Gizzy didn't recognize any of their faces. They clearly weren't Nose People Characters.

"This is bad…really bad! Altered will crumble without Alpha!" Hey, Gizzy thought he recognized that voice. It was just so familiar. Wait! Of course, it was Voice! Though it was incredibly odd for Gizzy to see him with a physical body.

"That's why we're here!" a figure in a brown waistcoat said. He wore a yellow tie. "Don't you believe my father can see into the future? I'm telling you, he can predict what will happen and tell us what we need to do!" He looked toward an older figure, presumably the father he'd just been talking about. "Voice, just join hands with us, and you'll see."

Voice breathed a deep sigh, then reluctantly held out his hands. The three of them linked together and all closed their eyes. Gizzy could see the tension in their expressions. A light glowed around the figures as they concentrated hard, squeezing each other's hands.

Then, suddenly, Voice let go, stood up with a smile on his face, and said, "I saw it! I believe! I believe! We just have to find the Chosen One."

"But it's not going to be that simple," the one in the waistcoat said. "You saw yourself in my father's vision that the Chosen One isn't from this planet. Finding him will be difficult. I'm not saying impossible, just difficult. We need to meet up with my contact and figure out how to get the Chosen One here."

"Which contact are you speaking of?"

"The one who can jump between planets. He can help us get to the Chosen One, and hopefully he can save us all. Just trust me on this."

The three of them nodded, shook hands, and Voice and the figure in the waistcoat walked away. The father looked up to the child, who stood and nodded.

"You know what to do, son," the father said.

Suddenly, the child put his hands together. Sparks shot from his fingers, and a light steam rose. Out of nowhere, a miniature cyclone started turning in his palm! Great gusts of wind blew through the cavern, and the miniature cyclone grew and grew into a hail of a storm.

Then...there was darkness.

Gizzy woke with a fright and sat up, which alarmed Betsy, who was actually worried about Gizzy's wellbeing. Gizzy slowly tried to make it to his feet, then stumbled and fell. He blinked several times, then closed his eyes again.

Betsy was worried about what the boy might do to him, and fearing for his life, he took off and left the pub behind. He had only stuck around to make sure the stranger wasn't dead, and even after the boy fell again, Betsy could still see his chest rising and falling, so he knew was alive and breathing, at least, though possibly seriously injured. Also, Betsy was unsure of what the stranger might try to do to him, and he didn't want to stick around and find out.

Gizzy finally stood and shook the dust off. He went behind the bar and found an old half-full jug of water. He pinched his nose, tilted the jug, and chugged. Only after he was done chugging did he taste the acrid swampy aftertaste. Disgusting!

Gizzy looked down at himself. He was really sore and had a mild headache, but other than a few minor scrapes, he was really doing OK. Nothing as bad as having a transwolf on top of you.

Oh no.

Suddenly he was reminded of how late it was. He looked through the gaping rectangular hole where the door had been before he had kicked it down. Gizzy saw nothing but blackness outside; clearly, time was up. He felt an intense pressure inside his body, an awful tingling, then he started to shake like he was having a seizure and fell on the floor, writing. The Canine was back for more.

Betsy had run from the Green Lageen as fast and far as his little stubby legs could carry him. Betsy stopped and looked around. He realized the stranger hadn't followed him and bent over, panting hard. After getting some of his breath back, Betsy reached behind his round torso and felt the outside of his dark shoulder bag to make sure the book was still there. Yes, he could feel its corners and weight. He still had it.

Betsy laughed. "Oh, that poor fool and his big fall. Pretty funny, really. He would have left if it were me! I know it! But still. Maybe he wouldn't have. Damn poor kid." He couldn't help but feel bad for the stranger. And Betsy wasn't some villain, he had always just wanted respect from the villagers and the creatures of the surrounding area. Having the book wasn't just about selling it for the money. With the power contained within its pages, Betsy could become enlightened on how to grow into a respectable troll, maybe by being covered in magic dust or he would possibly find the ingredients for special potions to make him revered among his companions and any new strangers he might come across. People would know his name all over Altered, and they wouldn't think of him as a failure and a loner and a being that no other creatures wanted to be around. He would be a success for the first time in his life. He would learn what it meant and how it felt to be truly respected. Redemption. Isn't that what all those who had fallen on hard times or done wrong truly wanted? And when he had obtained the secrets of the mystical book, he could sell it, thus passing on its knowledge and power, and that could make him enough money to live comfortably for the rest of his life. Then maybe he would even fix up the rundown Irish pub and rechristen it as the Green Lageen II. Betsy's Green Lageen and Beans. The Green Lageenenstein. The Green Lageen Canteen. Oh! That had a nice ring to it.

But then…what about the poor stranger who had knocked himself unconscious? That darn kid. He had fought so hard to find Betsy and seemed so intense and desperate to have the magical book. What if he really needed it? What if it was life and death?

Betsy stood torn between helping the stranger or returning back to his world of trolls with the book in his shoulder bag and the aim of finally becoming respected and admired. He worried that maybe the stranger would stop breathing or needed serious help. And Betsy really wasn't the kind of troll who would simply let someone die if he had the chance to save him. He knew it was the right thing to do.

Betsy was certain he should turn around and head back to the Green Lageen. He was determined to save the boy and become his hero, to start his brand-new life in this way, and maybe they could share—

A quick, excruciating pain shot through Betsy's body.

Sharp claws went through Betsy's back and came out through his chest. A trail of warm blood ran down his shirt, and he dropped to his knees. He tried to breathe but could only gurgle. A figure moved in front of Betsy, and for the first time in his life, Betsy was face to face with an eerie black wolf.

Betsy felt hollow, paralyzed. His pupils had vanished and turned his eyes completely black as more and more blood spewed out of him. The dark bag, now dangling from his shoulder, fell to the ground with the weight of the book.

The Canine breathed on the dying troll. Betsy looked up into the eyes of the wolf. The beast looked back at its victim in a deep exchange of so many emotions. Betsy stared hard with the last of his energy, the last of his life, and could see that poor boy trapped inside, innocent, almost pleading for forgiveness.

With his final breath, Betsy let out a small, pathetic cry, and said, "I…I can see your fear…" causing a tear to fall from the eye of The Canine.

Then Betsy fell forward and died against the beast.

The Canine gently shrugged off the body and set the corpse of the poor troll on the ground. Acting only on instinct, the beast hooked the shoulder bag over his neck, angry and confused, and ran as fast as he could deep into the dark wilderness.

The Canine ran through the forest at blazing speeds, Gizzy horrified at what he had done as the uncontrollable wolf and finding it so strange to be galloping on four legs and be so low to the ground. The eyes of unknown mystical beasts glowed in the dark as they watched the wolf run by.

Because of his sudden transformation into The Canine, Gizzy didn't have time to think about the odd, first-person dream he'd had while trapped inside the child's point of view. The thought that was now pervading his mind was that he was actually brought to Altered on purpose and for a reason. Voice had clearly *planned* to bring Gizzy here, but why? And what was in the psychic vision that the three beings had seen when they joined hands? What did it have to do with the child? Was it true that the cyclone the child had created in his hands was made purely to bring Gizzy to this planet? And if so, then what in the heck was the Prophecy, and what was the real reason Voice wanted Gizzy to go there?

He had run so fast and swift that he was soon close to the old shack where Gizzy would be safe for the rest of the night. He reached a giant hill in a meadow, slowed down to a stop, slanted his neck up to the glowing green moon, and howled into the clear night sky. The howl echoed throughout the land of Altered, scaring all the nearby creatures, who ran away and hid in fear. As The Canine, he was powerful and felt as if he owned this land. He looked up to the full moon in the sky and wondered if this would be his life from now on. Half the time as a teenage boy, lost and missing home, the other half as a super-powerful wolf that Gizzy could not control. As he looked toward the moon and the stars, he wondered if one of those blinking lights was Earth…his home was far, far away.

Gizzy, still trapped inside the wolf, began crying as he thought about what he had done to Betsy and what Betsy had said to him. How would Gizzy ever be able to control himself as The Canine? Though he was trapped inside, he needed to find a way to reduce the instincts and impulses of the beast, but how? He may never figure it out.

He thought again of being inside the child's perspective and of the psychic vision. Whether or not the vision was somehow related to getting him back to Earth, Gizzy was certain of one thing…that the Prophecy was of key importance to the guardians here on Altered and played a major role (and possibly his only chance) in getting back home.

The stars looked like beacons of hope for Gizzy's lost soul, while the shimmering green moon seemed to recreate a face with its scattered rocks, smiling down upon him like everything would be all right in the end. The moon shined its emerald essence while the shaken wolf looked back, Gizzy wondering whether or not he would ever see home again. He howled at the moon, seeking the answer he desperately needed.

He sat there for a long time as The Canine, waiting atop the hill in the meadow, looking at the moon in the mystical night sky. He could see night flowers blossoming all around and feel the thrumming of strange animals sleeping peacefully underground, their bodies pulsing with their sleeping breaths, safe from the dangers of the night. The beauty of being in another world was seeing the creations in a different light. He figured maybe life was about the journey ahead and what needed exploration. The sky taught Gizzy this, and even as a monster in another world, he still believed in it. Part Gizzy and part beast, he adored the night sky and all of its beauty. Not only was it a sign of hope but the opportunity for a journey. Anything was possible with the night sky, and Gizzy was a prime example of that.

Chapter Six

How To Summon A Fairy

Gizzy woke up atop the hill in the middle of the meadow, having forgotten the events of the previous night. When had he fallen asleep? He didn't remember that, either. But at least he wasn't eaten by any strange creatures while he slumbered! What luck! Also, he felt fortunate that his clothes had once again rematerialized.

Gizzy stood, scratching his head, and wondering why he didn't remember much of his time as a wolf. Then he looked down and saw the dark shoulder bag he had taken from Betsy. He opened it up and found the mystical book inside. The memory of last night was so hazy for him, though inside he felt a deep and strong sense of regret. All he was certain of was that he really wished he was able to control the beast! But what could he do?

Gizzy sighed, pulled out the mystical book, tossed Betsy's shoulder bag aside, and flipped through some pages. A slight wind blew, and Gizzy was reminded of the child with the cyclone on his palm. Had his dream been a reality that the world had let him tap into? And if so, why? How? Altered offered so many questions and very few answers. Gizzy felt so lost, confused, and alone. He missed the comfort of home so much. He wondered if his mother was doing all right.

Gizzy was hungry. Luckily, there were still a bunch of snap apples inside the red backpack. He set the book down and took off the backpack, opened it up, and ate the snap apples inside, which made him really thirsty. So he walked to a nearby creek and drank dozens of handfuls of clear, crisp water and thought of how good it felt to be nourished again. Maybe in contrast to the wild destructive desires of the beast, this replenishing of the healthy things felt even better than usual. Gizzy was grateful.

He walked back up the hill in the middle of the meadow and sat down with the book. The dark-red sun was slightly hidden behind some puffy clouds, and the day was warm and nice. Gizzy inspected the book. It had ribbed lining and a purple cover with a crudely drawn image of a fairy. The rough sketch looked like it had been done in pencil, and the fairy had specks of fairy dust falling from its wings. Gizzy flipped through the pages, and though the book contained lots of information about the fairy—origins, skills, variations—he only wanted to know how to summon it. Gizzy skipped through until he finally found a chapter called "How to Summon a Fairy."

A little way into the chapter, he found an entire page covered with a handprint symbol. Gizzy laid the book down in the grass and placed his hand on the print, then waited patiently. Waited. And waited. And waited a little longer. But nothing happened. He lifted his hand, finally giving up. Then he noticed fairy dust falling from his palm. His whole hand was covered in blue dust that had appeared as if by magic.

Gizzy blew the fairy dust off his palm and into the sky. As the little blue grains floated into the air, the most incredible thing happened—the dust formed a cloud and turned into smoke! Gizzy felt his heart lift with joy at the sight. These were the kind of moments he had hoped for when wishing for an adventure, and so far, this was turning out to be a good day. He felt a sense of joy for the first time in a while. And as the cloud dispersed, a small fairy emerged. The little guy was maybe a foot tall, had light skin, and bright white wings covered in blue dust that scattered like pollen every time he shook them.

He wore a tiny blue shirt and yellow leggings, with cute little white daps on his feet. His blue hair was tied in a bunch with a neat fringe covering his forehead. He opened his big blue eyes, and then the cute little fairy screamed as loud as he possibly could.

Gizzy took a few steps back, only for the fairy to fly up to him and hug him! Gizzy was shocked and now covered in blue fairy dust. He was really confused by the overly friendly fairy and stepped back a few feet. He hadn't been met with affection or much kindness on this planet, and he was a little wary of his newfound companion.

"You summoned me, my new master!" The fairy said, clearly excited about the prospect. Ultra-thrilled. Overjoyed. Maybe even a little overwhelmed because it seemed like he wanted to cry. "Ahem. Greetings! My name's Benji. I'm a fairy, as if that's not obvious enough, and I'm here to help you in any way I can!"

"Um, a fairy named Benji?" Gizzy said, watching the fairy float and beat his wings, light dust falling below.

Benji smiled at Gizzy, waiting to be told what to do.

"Uh, OK. Well, hello. My name's Gizzy, and I'm—"

"Gizzy!? That's a silly name for an NPC!" Benji fell to the ground, laughing hysterically, which released even more blue dust that puffed out of him with his little shaking belly. Gizzy was a little embarrassed at how flamboyant the fairy was, but he also found it cute and endearing.

"Wait...an NPC? I'm a human, I'm not an NPC!" Gizzy didn't have the traits of an NPC and was slightly offended. His nose wasn't *that* big!

"Wait, are you serious?" Benji stopped laughing and flew up to Gizzy's level. Shocked, Benji gasped and flew around Gizzy several times, looking him up and down and finally realizing that he was quite different from the other beings in Altered. "You're not from this world! And you're certainly not a Justment, either. No, no, no."

"No...I'm from the planet Earth, and I need your help. I'm cursed! I'm a transwolf now, and I was told that summoning you would somehow cure me."

Benji circled back around and hovered in front of Gizzy's face. "Summoning me *did* cure you! You will no longer change into a transwolf at night! You're free!"

Gizzy smiled. He was so happy to be free of the wolf and the wild instincts of the beast. Gizzy had felt a sense of relief and joy when Benji had come out of the book, and that must have been the release of the curse.

"Well...there is one thing," Benji said, looking a little coy. "You do have a kind of power inside you now."

"Wait, what? A kind of power? What do you mean?"

"You see that ant hill behind you?" Benji pointed to a little brown hill a few feet away. "Step on an ant."

"Why? I don't want to harm anything anymore, especially now that I'm free of the beast."

"Trust me. I'm here to help you, Gizzy. If you don't trust me, then how is this relationship ever going to work, huh? OK, then. Now, go over there and step on an ant, and you'll see what I mean about the power. A Justment I worked for ended up with this power after being in the same situation as you."

It was comforting to know that Benji had been involved with someone else who had gone through this same nightmare, and Gizzy couldn't help but wonder how that whole thing had ended. He was afraid to even think about the possibilities, let alone ask. So he decided to have faith in Benji and walked up to the little ant hill.

Then he hesitated. Could he really trust Benji? It didn't feel like he could truly trust anyone in Altered. Brayden seemed pretty OK, but the jury was still out on him. The only person Gizzy thought he might be able to trust was Voice, but if his bizarre dream was from a real occurrence, then Voice was misleading him, too, and that made Gizzy feel really unsettled. But then again, maybe the dream was only that, just a dream, and none of it had actually happened. On the other hand, Voice had saved Gizzy's life by shooting the great light at Woof, and he had also hooked Gizzy up with Benji, who had apparently helped cure the transwolf inside him. And without Brayden's help and patience and guidance, Gizzy wouldn't have ever gotten to Benji...OK. So maybe not everyone on this planet was so bad, and Gizzy was just being paranoid due to the random and peculiar circumstances. He needed to learn how to accept help and trust more. With that in mind, Gizzy put his trust in Benji and stepped on a stray ant trying to drag a tiny crumb up the hill.

Suddenly, a spark hit the dead ant, and gold dust, similar to Benji's fairy dust, glowed around the tiny ant body and flowed into Gizzy's foot. As Gizzy stepped back, the gold dust encircled his body.

"Benji! What the heck is happening to me!?"

Gizzy felt himself getting smaller and smaller. His body parts changed shape as his clothes disappeared. His limbs shrunk down, and his skin color turned from white to dark red. Why had he trusted Benji? What was happening to him?

Terrified, Gizzy continued to shrink, and he felt sharp pains as he morphed into a small creature. Eventually he was super tiny…well, the size of an ant. He looked into a small puddle of water on the ground to see his reflection, and he was surprised to find out that he *was* an ant! He had sharp pointers at the front of his mouth, six spindly legs, and a dry scaly shell around his body. His big black eyes started to swell with tears. He had gone from a terrifying wolf to a miniscule ant. He tried to look all around, but the blades of grass were so giant all around him that he had trouble seeing.

"Benji!" Gizzy yelled. "Benji, get down here right now!"

Benji flew down to the ground near Ant Gizzy and laughed. "You look so silly!" he said, and fell to the ground laughing again. Benji's voice sounded much deeper now that Gizzy was a tiny little thing.

"Look what you've done to me!" Gizzy yelled, surprised that he could still talk, being that he was now an ant. Then he started to notice something else. "Wow...I can talk? I couldn't talk as a wolf. This is amazing! I seem to have free will, too." Gizzy walked around on his six legs. He had never felt anything so strange. Being a tiny insect was so much different than being a wolf, which seemed at least closer to what a human was. "As a wolf I couldn't control myself," Gizzy continued. "And, Benji, this is fun and all, but can you change me back, please? I just want to be Gizzy again for a while!"

"I don't have the power to change you back...but you do! All you have to do is close your eyes and concentrate. Think really hard about being human again, and you'll change back to your regular self."

Gizzy closed his big black ant eyes and thought hard about his dark dreadlocks, his white skin, his blue eyes. Soon his ant body was encircled in gold dust. Gizzy grew bigger and bigger, and this time he felt no pain at all. It was almost as if his body had somehow gotten used to the changing already.

Once Gizzy was back to his old self again, he looked down and was happy to see that his clothes had reanimated. He always hated worrying about that part! But Gizzy was human again and happy about it.

"So, tell me about this whole 'becoming an ant' thing." Gizzy said. "What was that all about?"

"I told you that you had a new power, and this is it. You now have the morphing ability and can morph into any being you kill, either on purpose or on accident. But remember that if you do kill something, you must be close

90

enough that you're able to absorb the little shock and the energy. You gained this ability after becoming a transwolf, but it was dormant inside you. After you summoned me, you unlocked the power and blocked the transwolf part. Pretty cool, right? I'd say that's a pretty good exchange."

Gizzy smiled, thinking of just how much had happened to him in only four days. He was slightly overwhelmed, having been given this opportunity to go on the kind of adventure nobody else would ever experience. Who would believe him back in Houston? His mother, if she ever forgave him for his horrible words, would probably think he had gone crazy. All the people back home and the gang at T4T would probably think the same, but either way, Gizzy felt proud of his newfound spirit and confidence. He was learning so much and having new experiences all the time. Who could truly say that about their life and mean it? Well, he could! At least for now. And this strange world of Altered had given him this wonderful adventure…even if it was a little more altered than he could have ever anticipated.

"Sorry, Benji I'm just trying to absorb all this new information and all these sudden changes. Everything just happens so fast on your planet! Or maybe it's just my weird situation."

Benji flew up in front of Gizzy and slowly buzzed around him for a minute, dropping blue dust on his shoulders. "Here, that might help calm you down a little," Benji said. "And, um…I'm sorry."

Gizzy did feel a little better inhaling the dust and feeling it on his shoulders. "Thanks, Benji." Gizzy tried to shake off his worries and was determined to figure this thing out. "So, I can now choose to be whatever being I've killed, as long as I'm close enough to absorb its energy? Is that right?"

"Yep, you've got it."

"And you said something about someone else who went through this or something similar, right? Who would that be?"

"I can't tell you," Benji said, putting his hands on his tiny hips as he hovered.

Gizzy was disappointed. He needed answers.

"But I can show you!" Benji said.

"What?"

Benji flew toward the ground and looked through the little red backpack. Soon he pulled out Gizzy's compass and entered the coordinates X345 Y60 Z11. "Put the book in your bag, strap that baby on, and let's get rolling!" Benji said.

Gizzy felt a burst of energy and excitement. He was happy to begin his next adventure and meet this Justment to find out more about his new power. Worrying about the Prophecy slowly drifted from his mind as the duo headed off.

Chapter Seven

Dr. Shamas And Mr. Stryder

They arrived in a peaceful, calm meadow. Tall, skinny trees were all over the place. Too tall. Like, taller than any trees Gizzy had ever seen. As they moved along, Gizzy tried to think of a new nickname for himself. Apparently now he could no longer be The Canine, and maybe that was for the better. Since he now had the power to change into many different beings, why not call himself...the Transformer? Yeah, that sounded good!

Then Gizzy noticed Benji was snapping his fingers, trying to get Gizzy's attention. Benji pointed upward, and following Benji's gaze up a high climb, Gizzy spotted what appeared to be a giant dirt ball floating several feet over the edge of a cliff. What an incredibly odd and curious sight. It must have been a hundred feet up or more. Gizzy realized this must be where the Justment lived, and he wondered what in the heck someone was doing living inside a giant floating dirt ball with nothing but certain death far below? Before Gizzy could ask, Benji flew off toward the ball with the obvious intention of going inside.

"C'mon!" Benji shouted down to Gizzy, who was still waiting near the base of the climb. "What are you waiting for? Let's get up there!"

"The gap between the dirt ball and the cliff is too big...I can't just climb up there and jump that! And who in their right mind would jump from a cliff into a floating dirt ball in the first freaking place!?"

"Who said anything about jumping?" Benji laughed and continued upward. Confused but determined to trust in Benji, Gizzy followed up the steep climb. Step by step, rock by rock, Gizzy ascended higher, until he was finally near the lip of the cliff and too afraid to look down. He had a pretty big fear of heights and was proud of himself for having gotten this far.

"Are you OK?" Benji shouted down.

"I'm...I'm afraid of heights," Gizzy said. He cowered on the cliff keeping his body as close as possible to the rock surface to make sure he didn't fall. But when he reached his left foot up higher to get a better footing, the rock below slipped and gave way, falling to the ground far below. Gizzy tried to hold on, but his grip wasn't strong enough, and he slipped off the rocks and plummeted.

"Ahhhh!" Gizzy screamed, and he closed his eyes. He was certain he would be dead, kaput, gone from this world. That this would be the end of Gizzy...

At least...it would have been...if he hadn't summoned Benji.

Gizzy opened his eyes and found himself...floating! Well, technically he was still falling, but thankfully at a very, *very* slow rate. He was gliding down toward the ground like a hang glider.

"Benji, what's happening to me!?" Gizzy asked, as he floated down.

"That was going to be my surprise, but you ruined it!" Benji flew just below Gizzy and helped pull him back up before he hit the bottom. Once in place, Gizzy continued to climb the craggy surface again, laughing as he went forward. Gizzy could fly! Well, sort of. What an incredible life experience Gizzy was having, with so many strange and wonderful things happening to him. Gizzy put his feet and hands on the different jutting rocks and into the jagged cracks, climbing again in attempt to get high enough to board the giant sphere. He felt his fear of heights gradually diminishing the higher he went. Having conquered his fear of falling, it was as if his fear of heights was leaving him, too.

Out of nowhere, Gizzy started to wonder about the idea of home and if he even wanted to go back to his alcoholic mother who was probably certain by now that Gizzy had died in the cyclone and that his bones had settled somewhere in the Gulf of Mexico. Maybe being in Altered would give Gizzy a fresh start, a new challenge, something he had been dreaming about for some time. Hadn't he put a ton of effort into helping his mother, and what had she done for him? She had given birth to him and been an OK mother after that, but she hadn't done anything special for Gizzy, and she had been mentally absent for so many years, it was like he didn't even know her anymore, and maybe she didn't know him. Were they just strangers who had lived together? Gizzy only ever felt like some kind of nurse to her and never her son. He had badly wanted a relationship with her for so many years, but did he now? Was he better off this way? Were they *both* somehow better off this way? Maybe living in Altered wasn't exactly what he'd had in mind for an adventure and certainly wasn't an ideal existence, but at least it was unique and always offered excitement and adventure! Was Gizzy really thinking about staying here? It was pretty nice having an unlikely travel companion in Benji, and other than this bizarre dirt ball in the air, everything seemed to be heading in a better direction, and Gizzy was grateful for that.

At the top of the steep climb, Gizzy cautiously peered over the edge of the cliff. The sheer drop took his breath away. A fall from here in the real world would mean certain death. But then, this wasn't the real world, or at least not the world he understood. This was far from it. Although, this world was the "real" world to all those who lived in it and wandered through it. To the inhabitants of Altered, his world, Earth, would seem incredibly strange, unreal, and probably very dangerous.

Benji flew over the cliff top toward the dirt sphere, taunting Gizzy to jump. "C'mon, you know you can glide off the edge. You're safe! You can do it! Besides, you wanted to meet the one who's like you, right? Well, it's the only way in, buddy!"

"Uh, I know! Just give me a sec, will you? I need to think about it."

"What's there to think about?" Benji asked, smiled, and flipped around in circles in the air. "See, it's pretty easy to just fly and float around. No big deal."

"Easy for you to say. I've obviously never jumped off a cliff before."

"From what you told me on the way here, you survived a cyclone, pirates, and being attacked by wolves...and you're telling me you're afraid to jump off a measly little cliff?"

96

Benji smirked as Gizzy realized he had been through a lot and maybe even been through more dangerous situations than this. He stepped back to give himself space for a running start, then sprinted toward the edge.

"You got it!" Benji called out.

Gizzy knew that if he thought too much about this he would stop running, so he let his mind go blank as he churned his legs. When he got to the edge, he closed his eyes, planted a foot, and made the leap. Gizzy could feel his heart racing as he flew through the air, and then he suddenly started plummeting toward the ground again, where he would surely die.

Seconds ticked by as he fell. Endless time.

Then, all of a sudden he realized he was gliding, floating as if in outer space! He slipped through the air toward the sphere above the giant drop-off and looked over to find Benji, who was laughing as he flew beside Gizzy.

Gizzy felt euphoric and just couldn't help laughing along with him as they floated toward the dirt ball. Now Gizzy was having a wonderful time, and he did somersaults through the air and twisted and turned.

When they were nearly at the sphere, Gizzy closed his eyes, and he and Benji went through the cloud of dust and landed safely on top of the big sphere. This is when Gizzy realized the next dilemma—digging his way in.

Benji giggled as Gizzy tried to dig through the solid, packed mud with his bare hands. But then Benji was surprised to see that Gizzy was able to quickly make a sizeable hole in the roof, and when Gizzy loosened enough dirt, the hole caved, and Gizzy fell into the sphere. Dirt and tiny rocks followed for a few seconds before everything settled. Gizzy shook off the debris and stood. He looked up to the hole where Benji was looking down at him, a relieved look on his face.

Inside, Gizzy found a surprisingly tasteful interior with a safe, homely feel to it. Abstract sketches and paintings ran along the curved walls and somehow fit the décor. Finally, he saw a small bed with a figure lying on it under a blanket. A groggy face was peering out from under the blanket, and his eyes looked wild.

"Who goes there!?" his voice boomed. There was nowhere for Gizzy to run, so he just stood there on top of the pile of debris, hoping the figure would calm down.

But the Justment jumped out of bed with a wild look in his eyes and approached Gizzy. "Trespasser! What are you doing breaking in here!? And look at the damage you caused to my roof!" He lifted his hand as if to strike Gizzy.

"Wait, wait! Benji brought me here," Gizzy said, panicked, as he pointed up at Benji.

Benji flew down from the hole in the roof and slowly buzzed. "Hey there, old pal," he said to the Justment.

"Benji!" the Justment cried, with a sudden change of heart after seeing his old friend. The Justment lit up after looking at Benji and seemed to have a lot of love for the little fairy. "It's been so long! I'd love to chat, but you'd really better get going, and soon. Stryder's going to be here any minute! I can feel it!"

"Who's Stryder? I thought you lived alone," Benji said.

The Justment frantically put on a shirt. Gizzy looked him over. His face was covered in cuts, gashes, and scars, which gave him a rugged appearance, as though he had been in many battles. His dark eyes gave him a shady look, and Gizzy didn't trust him at all.

"But Dr. Shamas!" Benji said, flying over to hug him, covering him in blue dust. Dr. Shamas returned the hug, then casually wiped the dust off, as if this were an everyday occurrence. "I came all this way to introduce you to a new friend of mine. This is Gizzy, and he has the same power as you!"

Suddenly, Dr. Shamas's face went dark and scary again. "You gave him the power to morph!? Do you realize what you've done?" Dr. Shamas asked, in a deadly serious tone. "You need to leave quickly. Get out before he gets here, dammit! I can feel him coming!"

Dr. Shamas approached Gizzy and pushed him. "Get out, I said!"

Was there no way out of the dirt sphere? Gizzy couldn't see a door or window or any kind of opening except the one he had made in the roof.

"What the heck is going on here?" Gizzy asked, pushing Dr. Shamas off him. "We came all this way and risked our lives, and I'm not leaving until you tell me what's going on. We came all this way just to meet you!"

"Trust me, kid, you were better off being a vampire," Dr. Shamas said.

Vampire? Clearly, he had his facts wrong.

"I was bitten by a transwolf, not a vampire!" Gizzy said, annoyed and confused.

"A transwolf? But I became like this because I was bitten by a vampire, not a transwolf. This could change everything that has happened to me...or delay it..."

"What happened to you?" Gizzy asked, nervously. It was starting to seem like the power he had acquired might not be as promising as he had hoped.

"After I was bitten by the vampire, I started turning into a vampire every night without fail, so I had to leave my family and head off in search of a cure. Then I found Benji, who fixed my issue by giving me the morphing ability."

"I'm sorry that you were bitten by a vampire. Benji gave me the ability, too. I feel much better about it now. And that's why I wanted to meet someone else like me, to know that I'm not alone and that it's going to be OK," Gizzy said.

"Well, that's not the whole story and certainly not the worst of it. Because when the split personality kicks in, then you'll really be in trouble. It's entirely uncontrollable. It takes over everything! Benji never fixed the vampire inside me, instead it just stayed dormant, ready to unleash itself, building its power the more it waited. All it ever needs to take over is a simple trigger."

"This doesn't sound good at all," Gizzy said and gulped, as the realization of his true predicament began to dawn on him. A split personality? But life was actually starting to go better here on Altered! Why must something bad always happen as soon as things started going well?

"What do you mean about the trigger?" Benji asked, apparently not surprised at any of the other things Dr. Shamas had revealed.

"It's different for everyone, unfortunately I got unlucky, and mine's entirely random. I never know when it's going to go off, but I can feel it in my body, like an energy or a pulse. That's why I'm up here isolated and all alone. I decided it was safest not to return to a community. And I...ugh...oh, no." Dr. Shamas started coughing uncontrollably. "It's starting. It's happening now. You better leave! Go, get out of here while you can!"

"Gizzy, we need to go now!" Benji said, and flew up to the top of the sphere and out through the hole Gizzy had made. Then he quickly stopped in midair, remembering that Gizzy didn't have the ability to fly up, only glide down!

Gizzy was trapped inside the sphere, and the other half of the split personality was starting to come out. Dr. Shamas suddenly changed form, and the intimidating Stryder came out to play. Dr. Shamas's skin had gone from a pale white to a dark purple, his eyes glowed orange, and all of his hair disappeared.

Gizzy gasped, turned, and looked for a possible escape. There was a big curtain near one of the curved walls, and Gizzy yanked it open, hoping to find a door or window, but instead he found...a pile of skulls. Lots of them. There were far too many to count, and they appeared to be the shape and size of Nose People Character and Justment skulls. Gizzy realized that Stryder was a mad killer, and he was hungry for more.

Yikes! Gizzy could be next!

He turned back and looked at Stryder, a strange devil-like creature.

"The curse never leaves," Stryder said. Then he laughed in a maniacal way.

Gizzy was trapped with nowhere to go. The hole in the top of the sphere was much too high to reach. Then, suddenly he wondered if he could get out the same way he came in—by digging!

As Stryder slowly approached, salivating at the chance to make Gizzy his next victim, glow dust suddenly appeared around Gizzy, and he quickly morphed. He sprouted a tail, and as Gizzy dropped to all fours, black fur grew out of his body and covered him entirely. His teeth turned thick and sharp, and long razor claws grew from his morphed paws.

The Canine was back!

And like a canine, he dug and dug, as fast as his paws could work through the giant floating earth ball.

As Stryder reached down to choke The Canine, Benji distracted the devil-like creature by shooting blue fairy dust in his eyes, which blinded him long enough that The Canine was able to dig through the dirt floor until part of it crumbled, and he fell through and started gliding toward the meadow.

Benji quickly followed him through the hole as Stryder rubbed his eyes, then blindly swung his arms, hitting only the curved walls of his dirt-hardened sphere.

"What was all that about!?" The Canine asked Benji as they floated down. He was furious about what had just happened and also surprised that he could speak as The

Canine now. And not only that, but he seemed able to control the wolf a heck of a lot better than before.

"I'm sorry; I didn't realize he had turned so crazy with the split personality!" So he had known Dr. Shamas had an issue with the morphing ability, yet he led Gizzy to the dangerous sphere, anyway? Did he have no common sense!?

"I knew it. I knew you knew about him!" The Canine said.

They soon landed safely on solid ground.

"I'm done with you," The Canine angrily said. He decided that it would be best to de-summon the fairy, if that was even possible. He was tired of being used and lied to and tricked like this. Enough was enough.

"I'm sorry!" Benji said. "Please, please, don't be mad at me! I didn't know he had gotten so bad. Really!"

"Sorry isn't going to change this! I'm going to de-summon you."

"No! Please! It's so lonely inside that book; please, don't make me go back! I beg you! You don't know what it's like in there. It's dark, it's lonely. I spent thousands of years with only my own thoughts and no friends or family. Can you imagine? Please, take pity on me. Don't send me back to the pages!"

"What other choice do I have, Benji!? I trusted you, and you almost got me killed!"

"You're a transwolf!" Voice's powerful voice filled the air, scaring both Benji and Gizzy. "I see you managed to find the fairy, but you're still a wolf. What happened?"

103

"Voice! You're back! I didn't get to the book in time, so now the transwolf inside me is still able to come out, thanks to Benji!" The Canine sarcastically said, still upset with everything he had witnessed and discovered about his new powers.

"I said I was sorry!" Benji said, but The Canine wasn't listening. He hadn't minded the transwolf once he had gotten used to being within the beast and having a little more control over its actions, but the fact that the split personality would decide when it wanted to come out, according to some 'trigger,' was a horrible new development. Gizzy hated the idea of having a split personality now, and it was all because of Benji.

"Well, I have some good news, Gizzy! I found a way home!"

The Canine howled and jumped on all fours with joy. But he also felt a sense of uncertainty. Would he really want to return home? Should he stay here if he had the chance? But home was what he was most familiar with, and maybe he could return, see how it went, and find a way back to Altered, if it were possible.

Suddenly, gold dust surrounded The Canine. His tail shrunk back, and his paws changed back into hands. The black fur was shed onto the ground, and his clothes rematerialized. For whatever reason, turning back into a human caused Gizzy to think about the dream he'd had with Voice and the other beings inside the cavern, talking about the Chosen One. He wanted to ask Voice about it, but at this point, he was unsure if he could really trust him. Should he ask Voice about the dream?

"We need to talk about the Prophecy," Voice said.

"Prophecy!?" Benji was shocked to hear the Prophecy mentioned. He had heard rumors about it, and according to the rumors it was not a place anybody should attempt to find. "Gizzy, I don't trust this."

"Benji, who said you were even coming along?" Gizzy snarled at the fairy.

Benji lowered his wings. "Guardians are supposed to protect the Prophecy, so why would Voice want to take you to it? It doesn't make sense," Benji whispered.

"I do have a question for you, Voice: do you know anything about a child who can create cyclones?"

"No, nothing," Voice said rather quickly. It seemed rather suspicions, and Gizzy felt as though he was hiding something, but since Voice had no facial expressions, it was hard for Gizzy to really tell. "I don't know what you're talking about," Voice continued, and perhaps Gizzy's dream was nothing more than a dream. And maybe Gizzy was just reading too much into it, but it felt so real.

"OK, well what about a cavern with an odd yellow ore inside and something about a 'Chosen One'?"

"I honestly have no idea what you're talking about, Gizzy. Are you feeling OK? The Prophecy is your way home. It has magical energy that can take you back. That's the only relevant thing here. I thought you badly wanted to get home. What happened to that?"

"I don't know. The only thing I'm sure of is that I need to figure out how to de-summon Benji before I do anything else."

"No, you must go now if you're going to go at all. It's now or never, Gizzy! Think hard about your choice."

Gizzy had never heard Voice be so adamant before, and it seemed as if Gizzy had little choice but to go immediately. He was still uncertain about whether to stay or go, but Earth was his home, after all, and maybe it was time for this short but crazy adventure to come to an end. He had experienced more in these few days than most people do in a lifetime, and he was grateful for that. Always grateful.

"Well, Benji, I guess I'll put the de-summoning on hold for the time being. Looks like you're coming along. But I'll be keeping a very close eye on you, so no wrong moves or attempts to deceive me, got it? You've let me down already, and I don't ever want that to happen again!"

Gizzy walked away from Benji who could only accept defeat and follow Gizzy and Voice obediently, but secretly he felt happy that he got to join them on their quest to the Prophecy.

Gizzy was uncertain about finally heading home, but he figured this adventure had to end at some point, so why not sooner rather than later? He had been in this world long enough now.

Voice worried that Benji was getting in Gizzy's head and making him question the Prophecy and challenge Voice's motives. Maybe the boy understood too much and would eventually uncover Voice's whole plan. If Gizzy found out everything and diverted the course too much, the entire planet of Altered could be in jeopardy.

Chapter Eight

Deception

As they approached their final destination, it started to snow. Crisp white flakes fluttered down from the sky, just like on Earth. A simple reminder of how sometimes this strange and unforgiving world was not so different from home. Gizzy could see snowcapped mountains on the horizon. There was a small stone castle situated in the center. From such a distance, it looked like the castle had been somewhat destroyed and forgotten.

"What is that?" Gizzy asked, pointing.

"That...is the Prophecy. You're going home," Voice said.

Gizzy felt a sense of relief. Maybe some excitement, too. But he was also still uncertain. Who would understand him back home after all he had been through? What would his mother's condition be? Would anyone have missed him? Would he be essentially forgotten? If days had gone by here on Altered, had weeks, months, or years passed on Earth? Gizzy had read many science fiction books as a kid, and often transporting between worlds and dimensions changed the speed of time and the course of it.

Benji looked nervous, afraid, uncertain. He sensed something was really wrong, and as they moved closer to the seemingly abandoned castle, they were unaware that they were being watched. From a distance. From within the castle itself. The resident of this lost and once-magnificent castle smiled with his sharp, yellow teeth...Ratchet.

Gizzy trudged through the treacherous mountains with Benji flying at his side, shivering. They were trying their best to avoid the cold and howling wind, though it was impossible. At least Gizzy still had his trusty gray jacket, which he cinched tighter as they moved through the passes and winding turns.

After several freezing hours of chewing on snap apples and blowing warm air into their hands, Gizzy and Benji finally arrived at the castle, with Voice presumably somewhere in the air, though the duo hadn't heard from him in quite some time. The castle looked even worse up close. It appeared eerie and lost, clearly forgotten by time. Perched in the middle of nowhere, covered in frost, absent and in need of some good, positive company. Only one glass had seemingly survived and was beautifully stained, though covered with so much frost that the images were hard to make out. The rest of the brilliantly colored glass had been shattered and hung like broken icicles. Through the open top of the castle, an unsettling orange glow was visible, like the radiance from a giant fire. Gizzy assumed that someone was probably living here.

As Gizzy entered the castle and walked farther within its bounds, Benji flying at his heels, his intuition started telling him that this was perhaps not such a good idea, and maybe Benji was right about what he had mentioned back in the meadow. Gizzy looked back at Benji, who tried to give Gizzy a reassuring nod, but it was clear that he was deathly afraid. Gizzy felt a sense of sympathy for the poor little fairy. Had he been too hard on him before? Wasn't Benji just trying to help and offer his best?

Gizzy walked into a giant ballroom, its great roof opened to the elements. The walls were water-stained, chipped, and some had collapsed. Every painting along the walls or on the floor was destroyed, their surfaces scratched to pieces or graffiti covering their once-beautiful exteriors.

The duo passed through the ballroom and entered a dark corridor. The word *LUCK* was written on the wall in a dark-red substance that was most certainly…blood. Gizzy wondered why *LUCK* was written on the wall inside this mysterious castle. What could it mean? Gizzy looked at Benji, who only shrugged.

"Well, Voice. We've come all this way now, so what am I supposed to do to get home?" Gizzy asked as quietly as he could. He didn't feel secure being here and didn't want to wake any strange creatures that might be stirring in such a dark and seedy environment.

No answer from Voice.

Gizzy turned around to see Benji, looking truly frightened. Maybe this really wasn't a good idea, but Voice said they *had* to come here immediately, that it was Gizzy's only chance to go home.

"Benji, are you OK?" Gizzy asked, reaching his hand out to the little fairy, who was floating a few feet away at Gizzy's chest level.

"I'm…I'm afraid," Benji said very softly. He badly wanted to return to the main lands of Altered but had agreed to accompany Gizzy to show his commitment and that he never meant him any harm. Benji also wanted to make sure his new friend was OK because he cared about him.

Gizzy moved his hand a little closer to the cowering fairy, and Benji reached out and touched the offering. The physical connection made him feel a little bit better.

"OK now?" Gizzy asked.

"A little better," Benji said, and he gave a half smile.

"Good," Gizzy said. "Now. Voice, are you there? Voice?" Gizzy looked around the castle, but again there was no answer. "Voice!" Gizzy shouted, as he was starting to become frustrated. "What did you make us come all this way for!?"

Benji quickly jumped forward and tried to cover Gizzy's mouth. "Shhh!" When Benji uncovered Gizzy's mouth, neither of them dared to move an inch. They could both sense another person in the room, and they looked up to the second floor to see an ominous dark shadow of a being. All they could clearly make out were the dark black eyes looking down at them.

"Go!" Gizzy shouted, and he took off down the dark corridor and passed through the giant ballroom with Benji flying at his side.

The dark figure lifted his right arm, then punched his fists together, causing the ground outside the entrance of the castle to collapse just as Gizzy was getting close to the big open doors.

Gizzy was trapped inside the castle with nowhere to go!

Benji had flown through the doors and was hovering over the giant dark chasm that now stretched across the outside entrance. "The stairs!" Benji yelled to Gizzy. "Run up those stairs!"

Gizzy ran up the decrepit stone stairs, and many of them cracked and broke off as he did. He stumbled a few times, but put his hands down on the cold stone as he pushed forward. Soon he made it to the top of the stairs.

"Now what?" Gizzy yelled to Benji.

No answer.

"Benji! Damn, you! You've deserted me, too!?"

Gizzy suddenly noticed the outline of Benji hovering outside a mostly broken stained-glass window.

"Break the rest of the window out, and use your new gliding ability. It's your only chance! That freak with the dark eyes is coming this way. I can see him crossing through the ballroom, and he looks aaaaannnngrryyy!"

Gizzy knew he couldn't punch through the glass without cutting up his hand, so he looked around. The broken stones from the stairs! He went down a few steps and collected some stones from the stairs and ran back to the cracked window. He threw a few of the smaller stones through parts of the glass, then took a bigger stone and bashed the remaining pieces out. He turned back to see the shadow of the dark figure coming out of the ballroom and knew he had little time left. Gizzy took a step up to the window sill, perched himself as carefully as he could with his heart racing, and stood for a moment, high up over the deep, dark abyss that now ran around the outside of the castle like an endlessly deep moat.

111

"You can do it, Gizzy! Just think of how you jumped the gap to the dirt ball!" Benji said, trying to give Gizzy some confidence.

"I didn't make that jump!" Gizzy yelled back.

"You know what I'm getting at. Just jump already! He's almost got you!"

Gizzy breathed in deep, closed his eyes, and leaped out of the castle window, igniting his gliding ability just at the height of his jump so he would be able to gain the most distance while gliding down and hopefully miss the torn-open ground.

And he made it!

When his feet touched the ground, Gizzy started to run as fast as he possibly could with Benji by his side.

"You were right, Benji, this was a trap! I should have believed you and trusted in you," Gizzy said, panting as he ran. "And I'd have been a goner if it weren't for you helping me again, so thank you."

Benji smiled as he flapped his wings hard. The cold air was stinging their faces.

"A few minutes of running, and we'll be in the clear," Gizzy said.

Then, he suddenly jerked to a stop. Gizzy was unable to move.

Benji slammed on the breaks and doubled back. "Gizzy? C'mon, let's go!" Benji waited for Gizzy to move, but he couldn't. He was frozen to the ground.

"I...I can't! I can't move my body!" Gizzy said, panicked. As Gizzy contemplated his immobility, his body started rotating on its own, moving him back in the direction of the castle. He tried to speak, but now that was impossible, too. All he could was think and panic.

Ratchet approached with a smile on his face. He opened his mouth and spewed forth a horrible noise, speaking in Greenbloodian, a language Gizzy still didn't understand. Gizzy had heard that same sound on the night he had arrived in Altered and wondered if this creature had been wandering outside the shack that night.

Gizzy's eyes were somehow forced closed, and he started to drift off to sleep against his will.

"Gizzy! Gizzy, no! Gizzy!" Benji's voice grew quieter and quieter until Gizzy was finally asleep.

A loud horn blew. Gizzy woke with a start and prepared to be attacked by the red-skinned beast coming at him. But then he noticed he wasn't in Altered anymore. He was...back on the cruise ship! The horn that had roused him from sleep must have come from up on the deck.

Suddenly, Gizzy started to move, but he wasn't controlling it. His eye level was low again, and he felt short. He soon realized he was trapped inside the child once more. The child opened the door and walked down the hall. It looked like nobody else was on board. The halls were empty, and the only noise was coming from the ship.

The child went up a flight of stairs and exited through a door that opened up on the side of the deck. He walked over to the handrail and looked out at the horizon, offering such a beautiful view of the world. The sun was setting on the other side of the deep blue ocean. Seagulls flew by, and fish swam happily down below.

The child soon started to walk again like he was on a mission, and Gizzy thought about how odd it was that he had been trapped inside the child before, had been trapped inside a wolf, had turned into an ant, had been utterly frozen with no ability to control himself, and was now trapped inside this child again. It was always such a strange feeling to be entirely controlled by something else, or even partially controlled, as when he initially became The Canine. At least now when he transformed, he could control most of his actions and talk.

The child walked into the bar, but nobody was there. Not a bartender or a waitress or a hostess or even a single person having a drink. Odd. The child went through some swinging doors, but no one was back there, either. He started walking through a big, long kitchen and spotted another door, this one partially opened. There was clearly an office back there, and as the child walked closer, Gizzy could hear voices and had the urgent sense that the child was not supposed to be there. The child must have realized it, too, and quickly hid in a cabinet filled with stainless steel pots and pans.

Soon, footsteps walked past the hiding place, then the swinging doors flapped. The child left the tiny space and followed into the bar. The beings had settled in a booth in the corner, and the child crouched down behind the bar and watched them by peeking his head around the side where waitresses normally came up to put in their drink orders.

When they talked, Gizzy immediately recognized the voices as being the same ones from his previous dream, and one of them most certainly belonged to Voice. The second being was also from his previous dream and was still wearing the long waistcoat. What Gizzy didn't understand was why Voice and the one in the waistcoat were on the ship in the first place. Maybe they really, truly did have something to do with the cyclone!

"Everybody's off the boat except for Gizzy, and he's fast asleep on a lounger."

"Excellent. It's only a matter of time before everything falls into place. The cyclone should arrive any minute now. Go and make sure he doesn't wake up or move from the top of the deck. We need to make sure he's in the main path of the cyclone when it hits, otherwise he might not arrive in Altered, and all this would be for nothing."

Suddenly, Voice looked over and saw the child poking his head around the side of the bar. They jumped up in surprise and quickly ran over.

"Aurona! How did you get in here!?" Voice grabbed the child by the arm and pulled him from behind the bar.

"I followed you! I created the cyclone and started it a few miles away, like you said. And I can jump into it, too!"

"No, that's very dangerous, and we might never find you again!" The one in the waistcoat said, face to face with Aurona.

Suddenly, there were movements up above.

"Gizzy," Voice said. He grabbed Aurona's hand and quickly pulled him out of the bar with the one in the waistcoat close behind. They stepped outside and climbed a set of stairs to the top deck, where Gizzy had been fast asleep but was now looking at a gigantic wooden ship that had docked next to the cruise ship.

Voice looked confused as to why there was another ship so close. They stealthily looked on without Gizzy noticing them. The second ship was rather large and had several thick masts and long, wide sails. Several cannons pointed out of little square windows, and a controlled fire blazed in the center of the rig in a circular pit. At the very top of the mast, just above the crow's nest, a giant black flag with a skull and cross bones snapped in the breeze. Pirates.

Aurona, Voice, and the one in the waistcoat watched Gizzy argue with the pirates. The sky had turned quite dark as the cyclone was clearly approaching from the north.

Suddenly three anchors hit the edge of the top-deck railing, and thirty seconds later, three young pirates climbed aboard the cruise ship—it was Clayton, Brandon, and Hugh. The angry pirates showed up at just the wrong time, because the cyclone was starting to really pick up speed and was whipping wind and rain only about a half mile away.

"Who are those people?" Voice whispered, clearly recognizing that his plan wasn't going so well.

Hugh, being an excellent captain by now and a master manipulator, had convinced the easily persuaded Clayton and often-dastardly Brandon to help him steal the classic replica pirate ship from Galveston's Madlock Maritime Museum. He had them all dress the part of old-fashioned pirates, but then didn't know what to do once they had the ship and were cruising around the gulf. Hugh had a spark of genius after seeing the halted cruise ship and decided it would be a great idea to commandeer the ship and rob everyone on board. He figured it would be an easy way to make some money *and* have fun doing it! But, unfortunately for the pirates, they were about to embark on an altered adventure along with poor Gizzy.

"Arrghhh!" Brandon yelled at the nearly empty cruise ship. "We've come for the treasure! Nobody will get hurt unless you—wait, where the heck is everybody?"

Brandon, Clayton, and Hugh looked around, but no one was there…except for Gizzy, who looked incredibly confused and tired from his recent nap.

"Guys!?" Gizzy immediately recognized his old friends.

"Gizzy!?" Clayton was shocked to see his old friend and felt very awkward now. "It's…um…good to see you…"

Aurona watched his handiwork as the cyclone whirled toward the cruise ship under all the dark clouds that had now covered the sky. Soon, Gizzy and the three pirates were swept up in the swirling winds and rain, and the Gizzy trapped within Aurona wanted to scream out to his old self and prevent him from falling into the trap of the cyclone, but there was nothing he could. He felt entirely helpless and miserable. There was nothing he could do to stop the fate of his former self.

"We need to go now before we're left behind!" Voice said, and then he linked hands with Aurona and the one in the waistcoat. They all jumped into the cyclone, where they were tossed and flipped and turned in wild circles until an electric pulse shot out of the cyclone in a thunderous burst, and everyone was gone, teleported back to Altered, and both ships splintered apart into thousands of pieces.

"Gizzy...Giizzzzyyy...Gizzy!"

Gizzy woke up, feeling exhausted and confused. Where was he? He looked down and realized he was back inside his own body again and felt really thankful. Man, it was tough constantly being trapped inside other beings.

Benji had spent the better part of an hour tugging on Gizzy's jacket and buzzing around his face, trying desperately to wake him.

"Gizzy, you're awake! You were having a bad dream. You kept flailing your arms and babbling."

It seemed the mystery of the cyclone and the truth behind how Gizzy came to Altered was slowly falling into place. Gizzy realized that sometimes, when randomly dreaming, he could see past events through the child's perspective. Gizzy was now certain that he was in Altered for a very specific reason beyond chance and chaos. It was also clear now that the pirates, his old friends, were never supposed to have boarded the ship and ended up on Altered entirely by accident. And Voice had clearly wanted Gizzy here and had asked Aurona to create the cyclone to bring about his transport, but why? What significance was Gizzy to the beings on Altered? He was only a regular teenage boy, after all.

Benji flew away from Gizzy to give him some space. Gizzy looked around, realizing he was in some kind of prison.

"Where are we now?" Gizzy asked.

"I'm afraid we're in a prison cell deep below the floors of the castle. Ratchet, that muscular red beast, carried you here, and I secretly followed him. I hid in that stack of hay in the corner until he locked the cell door and left."

"Good thinking, Benji," Gizzy said. "And thanks for being there for me."

Benji's wings fluttered a little faster as he hovered a few feet from Gizzy.

"I...I had another really weird dream, but it felt so real, just like the last one!" Gizzy stood up, trying to find his balance. He thought about the strange voodoo magic that had been placed on him and had made him unable to move when he was trying to run away. Gizzy felt like he was going to vomit, lost his balance, and fell back to the ground. "But I don't feel like it was just a dream, Benji."

"That sounds really intense!" Benji said. "And I'm really sorry about what Ratchet said to you back there, too."

"Wait, you can understand him?" Gizzy asked, looking shocked.

"Yeah, I can understand and speak a little Greenbloodian. Ratchet's the Earth Guardian. It seems to me that he's working together with Voice, and now all of a sudden they don't seem to want you to get to the Prophecy! Which I find odd, because didn't you say that Voice was trying to help you get to the Prophecy so you could return home?"

"Right! None of this makes any sense! I didn't even know the stupid Prophecy existed until Voice told me about it. So why even tell me about it if he was just going to betray me, lead me straight into a trap where this Ratchet freak could capture me, and stop me from getting there?"

"That's what I've been wondering since you've been in la-la land. Well, it might not make any sense, but we still have to get the heck out of here!" Benji said. Then he flew between the bars of the cell. "Listen, just after Ratchet dumped you in here, I heard him say that he was going to execute you for treason because you were trying to get to the Prophecy. Shouldn't he be punishing Voice for telling you about the Prophecy in the first place? And then attempting to guide you there? I don't know, it just all sounds so strange to me. I know I pop in and out of an old book a lot and have been stuck inside those pages for thousands of years, but this really doesn't add up for me, big guy."

Gizzy sat quietly for a while, contemplating what Benji had just said. Executed for treason? What had Gizzy done to deserve all of these crazy antics and misguided beings? He was constantly being judged and pulled in different directions. He just needed to stop and breathe, but there was never a good chance for it and certainly never a chance to actually relax. He needed a peaceful vacation from his adventure. He was certain of that.

"You're definitely right, Benji; we need to get out of here as soon as possible! I haven't come all this way to be murdered by some big crazy freak! And I'm not going to rot in some crappy jail cell, either! Now, how are we going to get me out of here?"

"Well, I can easily fit through these bars, but a human can't!" Benji said and sighed, almost giving up hope.

But wait! That gave Gizzy an idea. "You're right, a human can't fit through there, however…" Gizzy laughed, closed his eyes, concentrated really hard, and suddenly, gold dust covered his entire body, setting him aglow. Then he morphed into a little red ant.

"You're a genius, Gizzy!" Benji's spirits shot through the roof when Gizzy transformed.

As an ant, Gizzy was able to simply walk through the bars. The world was huge as an ant, and looking up from that little height gave Gizzy such a new and interesting perspective. The iron bars looked like huge Roman columns, and the dust on the floor was like walking over a sandy beach.

Benji landed on the ground in front of Gizzy, got down on his knees, and held out an open palm along the ground. "Gizzy, walk onto the palm of my hand, and I'll fly us through the window."

Benji's voice sounded deep to Gizzy as the ant. "Which window?" Gizzy asked.

Benji pointed to a cracked window along the far stone wall. "That one there. I bet I can make it. Come on, hurry!"

Gizzy continued walking forward toward Benji's open hand. "My six ant legs can't move *that* fast, you know! And I've only been an ant twice and only for a few seconds, so lay off!"

Benji laughed, waited for Gizzy to crawl onto his palm, then scooped him up, flew to the cracked window, and squeezed his way through and out into the cold, open air.

Benji flew Gizzy as far away as he could from the derelict castle before he landed and Gizzy turned himself back into a human.

"I can't believe we got out of that!" Gizzy said with a smile on his face. By now they were safely away from the snowy mountains, and Gizzy was impressed with how fast and far Benji had taken him. Benji hugged Gizzy with relief.

"I can't believe Voice betrayed me like that," Gizzy said. "The Prophecy must be even more important than I'd imagined. It must mean a great deal to the guardians, too, if they're keeping it this much of a secret and willing to kill anyone who dares to get there."

"I agree, but I really don't know anything about it. I'd heard of it, but I often thought it was just a myth. It's kind of cool to know that it's real, but it's also a little scary to think about going there. Hey, you said something about a dream?"

"Oh yeah! That dream I had...it felt so real. This wasn't the first time where I had a dream like that, either. Before I summoned you I'd experienced something similar, where I was dreaming but witnessing what I thought was a true event, only I was stuck in the viewpoint of a small child."

"I have no idea what you're talking about," Benji said and laughed. "So what happened in the recent dream? Were you here or on your own planet? Did you know anyone in the dream?"

"I was on a cruise ship on my own planet, and there was a cyclone created by the child. The ship was attacked by pirates. And I know Voice was involved, because he was in the dream and had a body and everything. And he clearly ordered the child to make the cyclone to get me to Altered!"

Before the duo could say another word, the ground beneath them started rumbling.

"Oh no," Gizzy said.

The earth shook and cracked open, and the duo fell in. Gizzy quickly found control and glided down into the dark cave, as Benji flew beside him.

"Benji, what do we do!?" Gizzy yelled.

"We hope for the best, my friend! We hope!"

A scream of anger rang throughout the crumbling castle. "How could this have happened? I was just with him!" Ratchet screeched.

"You were supposed to have this dealt with by now. You said you could take care of it! And I come back to find that you've let Gizzy escape!?" Voice said. "And what about the crazy little fairy? Did he escape, too? Or did you roast him over the fire for dinner, you big foolish baboon!?"

"Stop fussing, for crying out loud! We're guardians. We can just track him with our location ability!"

"That's the problem...I just tried, and I can't! Something's blocking my ability to locate him. He must be surrounded by Lucky Ore, but how could he have reached anything like that so quickly? And besides, he doesn't know anything about our tracking abilities, so he couldn't have ended up anywhere like that on purpose. It doesn't make sense."

Angered, Ratchet picked up a giant rock and threw it at the very last remaining frosted window, shattering it. "Well, you better go and find him somehow, Voice, otherwise you're not holding up your end of the agreement. We said the location of your body for the boy. So go find him or you're never getting your body back!"

Voice, angered by Ratchet's threat, had finally had enough of his blackmailing. "I'm sick and tired of this, Ratchet! You know how much having my body again means to me. I delivered Gizzy to you. That was our deal. I took care of my end of the deal, so don't blame me for your mistakes! I'm going to ask you one more time to tell me the coordinates of my body, and if you don't give them to me, I'll tell the other two guardians about how you've been blackmailing me and what a stinking, awful, horrible job you've been doing as guardian."

Ratchet gulped. He loved his position as a guardian, and at the same time he was deathly afraid of Inferno, the Fire Guardian, and the wrath he could bring down on those who disappointed him. Ratchet wasn't too worried about Letvia, who had always seemed loving and kind, but Inferno was tough as nails and already had a sharp dislike for Ratchet and didn't think he deserved to be a guardian.

"OK, fine. Fine! The coordinates are X44, Y100, and Z299. I'll find Gizzy and take care of it. I just have to figure out which patch of Lucky Ore is nearby and go there."

"I don't care what you do, just stay out of my business, and leave my plans alone," Voice said before disappearing.

"We'll see about that," Ratchet said, walking out of the open castle doors into the frigid mountain air.

Gizzy landed softly at the base of the underground cavern, which was illuminated by some kind of weird light coming from the walls. He figured the cave was long and probably full of googly-eyed monsters. Gizzy reminded himself that he just needed to survive, and darn if he wasn't super hungry again. Too bad his little red backpack was out of snap apples.

Benji looked over at Gizzy and laughed. "We're safe down here, friend! Trust me on that one."

"What do you mean? We're stuck inside a cave that probably has thousands of hideous monsters that I don't even want to think about right now!"

"This is Lucky Ore, Gizzy! Monsters are afraid of it, and guardians can't detect anything within the range of the light of the Lucky Ore, so you're good. We're safe at last!"

Gizzy stepped deeper into the cave. The Lucky Ore glowed so bright and illuminated the entire cavern. Suddenly, Gizzy recognized this place. It was the location of the first dream he'd had of the child creating the cyclone in his palm while the three beings talked among themselves—Voice, the one with the long waistcoat and yellow tie, and the father. Had fate brought Gizzy to the cavern, or would this place somehow mark the end of his incredible journey?

Chapter Nine

Lucky Ore Cavern

Gizzy and Benji were forty feet underground and exploring the caverns for a way out. They noticed that the different yellow glows of the Lucky Ore were all connected like a series of veins that ran along similar paths toward the center of the cavern. Gizzy suggested they follow the veins to reach the center of the cave, and soon they made it, only to find a being sitting cross-legged on the craggy ground. He had long hair, ragged clothes, and his skin was dirty. It took a second to recognize that this place must have been his home. There was a small fire going near the cave wall.

As Gizzy and Benji carefully approached, Gizzy suddenly realized this was the same figure from his first dream, the one he had figured was the father to the one with the long waistcoat and yellow tie.

The being opened his eyes and quickly turned in their direction. "Ah, Gizzy! I was wondering when you'd get here!"

Gizzy was shocked. "How do you know who I am?"

"Oh, my boy! I can see into the future quite well. Sometimes the visions are murky, other times I see things crystal clear. I've really wanted to have a chat with you and been hoping you'd show." He walked over to Gizzy and reached out for his hands. "I'm not here to harm you, only to advise you. Please trust in me and remember that." Then he released Gizzy's hands and walked back toward the center of the cave and sat on a little rug, where the Lucky Ore's veins seemed to intertwine into one large energetic point. "My ability to see into the future makes me a very sought-after resource for the four guardians. However, because of some highly...coincidental circumstances, I disagree with some of what the guardians do or stand for and refuse to let them have access to me and my powers. That's why I live down here, alone. The Lucky Ore gives off a charm that somehow disables the guardians' ability to track anything within a short distance of their golden glow, and none of the guardians know this place exists. At least for now."

"This is incredible," Gizzy said, thrilled to have found the Lucky Ore Cavern, as he had been looking for a safe haven for a very long time, and this seemed like the perfect place. With Voice seeming more untrustworthy and Ratchet looking to execute him, this golden cave might be the saving grace he had been looking for. But Gizzy also realized he couldn't stay underground forever if he truly wanted to go home, even though the idea of staying or going was a continual toss-up for him, a notion he couldn't stop wrestling with.

Benji flew up behind Gizzy's shoulder and fluttered there, clutching the thin fabric of his jacket to settle his uneasiness. Gizzy could feel his hand shaking. He really was a worrier!

"So, you said you can mostly see into the future, but can you tell me what that means, exactly?" Gizzy asked.

"This planet is filled with beings who have supernatural abilities, like myself and my two sons. I have the ability to often see into the future, and my oldest son can create voodoo spells and types of darker magic. We have the blood and energy of the Power-Borns."

"Power-Borns? That's interesting!" Gizzy pondered the idea of powers for a moment and how after being on this planet he was more powerful than he had ever been. Then he asked, "If you can see into the future, may I ask if you see me getting home? Or do you see me staying here, either by choice or because there's no other option?" This had easily been the biggest question weighing on Gizzy's mind, and he had been wanting to ask it ever since first dreaming of this being who had the ability to see into the future. He had also said that he had two sons, yet he only mentioned his oldest. Was his oldest son Aurona, who had created the cyclone that had thrust Gizzy and his old friends out of Earth and into the new world of Altered? It sure seemed like voodoo magic to Gizzy, whatever it was.

"No. I don't foresee you going home."

Gizzy heaved a deep, sad sigh. The tightness in his chest surprised him. Maybe he had wanted to get home more than he had realized? He wondered what it would be like if he was truly stuck here forever.

"Let me clarify that statement. I don't foresee you going home, at least not while I'm alive."

"That's a pretty important part to leave out, don't ya think?" Benji whispered into Gizzy's ear. Gizzy gave him a light nudge to hush him up.

"And if you're wondering…yes, you do need to go to the Prophecy, and as soon as possible."

"What *is* the Prophecy?" Gizzy asked. "Everybody keeps talking about it, the Prophecy this and the Prophecy that, but nobody will tell me anything about it! Voice says it's the only way home, Ratchet wants to kill me for trying to get there, Benji wasn't even sure if it existed—"

"Hey, leave me out of this!" Benji said, flying around Gizzy and poking him in the chest.

"Well, you said you didn't know if it was real or a myth," Gizzy said.

"Grrrrr." Benji gave Gizzy a dirty look, then flew back behind him.

"I'm sorry, Gizzy, but I can't tell you that, either. But if you play your cards right, I can guarantee you that in the future you'll find out from someone else. Just not from me. I really am sorry. You probably feel like you're being pulled all over the place."

"Ugh. You could say that again. Look, is there anything you *can* tell me? About the present, the past, the future? Anything?" Gizzy was clearly getting frustrated.

"What's your name, old-timer?" Benji asked, feeling a little braver now that Gizzy had let off some steam.

"My name's Gypsy." Gypsy gave Benji a genuine smile. "And Gizzy, some information I can offer you is that in order to get to the Prophecy, you need to be in possession of four keys. My son will soon meet with you and help you collect them, but the most I can tell you beyond that is that the first key is buried with Barath, who was one of the original guardians."

"Barath?" Gizzy was feeling confused and overwhelmed. Was he being forced into yet *another* quest to find the mysterious Prophecy? Was this thing even *real*!? *Hello*!? Sheesh!

"Wait," Benji said, arms folded. "So, what happened to Barath, then?"

"Yeah, what happened to him?" Gizzy asked.

Gypsy gestured for Gizzy to sit down on the spare rug, and he reluctantly did. His knees and ankles were aching from so much running and climbing over the past few days that getting into a cross-legged position was hard on him. If he ever got home, he swore he would take up yoga!

Gypsy spent the next half hour lecturing Gizzy and Benji about the big war, the death of King Alpha, how his body split into the four elements and were absorbed by the beings who were closest. He talked about how important it was to maintain the balance of the elements in Altered and how the slightest absence of a guardian would rupture the harmony of the planet. He told them about how the fire element was too much for Barath and that he had murdered Elizabeth. That her sister took on her element, and Inferno was chosen to embrace the fire, as he was already the Champion of Hell.

When Gypsy was finished talking, he sat in silence, Gizzy and Benji staring back, wide-eyed. He gave them time to let it all sink in.

Then Gizzy said, "Wow...thank you for telling us the history of your planet. Can I ask...where is King Alpha's body now?"

"Buried in his tomb at the Jungle of Hope. As the king, he had strong magical powers, too, but they were very different from Power-Born magic. The big secret about King Alpha is that if he's touched by the Chosen One he'll come back to life!"

"And that's another thing! I keep hearing about this 'Chosen One.'" Who is it? Is it a male or female? A Justment, an NPC, a crazy flying fairy?" Gizzy asked.

"Some say the king had a son who has now been lost to our history. That so many years ago he chose to give his son away in the hopes that the child could live a normal life without the constraints of royalty, war, dealing with the elements and great powers. He is said to have given the boy to Divine, who had been a confidant and close friend to King Alpha and his wife, but the son hasn't been seen since. Some say *he* is the Chosen One...but no one knows for sure. And it's possible that the touch of the Chosen One is only a myth and would do nothing to bring back the great King Alpha. Apparently, the son doesn't even know he's the prince of Altered. We tried having Alpha's wife, Jem, touch him in the hopes that she could bring him back, but it was of no use. Nothing. Our only hope for the king's return is to find the Chosen One, and we've been searching for years."

"That's some pretty heavy stuff," Gizzy said. "But thank you for telling us. I feel I know so much more about Altered now and all that you've been through."

"Thank you, my boy. Now, enough about the past. Let's talk about the future and how to get you back home. In order to do so, if that's something you still desire, you need to get to the Prophecy...but remember, to open the Prophecy, you need to find those four keys. I can give you the coordinates where you can find the first key, buried in the Dormancy Catacombs. Do you have a compass?"

Gizzy handed over his compass, and Gypsy put in some coordinates for him to track.

"Dig up the key and protect it. Each key is a special item that belonged to one of the original guardians when the Prophecy was first created—Barath's Hammer, Elizabeth's Locket, Voice's Aura, and Witch's Shield."

Gizzy nodded, taking the compass back from Gypsy as he stood, looking for an exit out of the cave. "Oh, my boy...take a left behind me, straight down, and you'll find a ladder up to the quickest exit. Be sure to close the trap door and cover it up with lots of dirt when you leave. I don't want the guardians or any other being to find the secret entrance!"

Gypsy hugged Gizzy.

"What was that for?" Gizzy asked, puzzled.

"You never know...this could be the last time we see each other."

"Oh...will it be?"

"Ha...you'll have to find that out for yourself...in the future," Gypsy said and laughed.

Gizzy and Benji moved toward the exit.

"Before I leave, I'd really like to know...what's inside the Prophecy?"

Gypsy turned around and smiled. "Home," he said.

∗∗∗

Thousands of miles away from any civilization, perched on the side of snowy Mount Kaivoo, far from Ratchet's castle, stood a lonely figure, head down, eyes closed, as if he were part of the colossal rock face surrounding him. The consciousness that had formed in the air around the body was suddenly absorbed, and they forged into one. Then, a pair of vivid blue eyes opened, and looked out from behind a shadow-gray mask with blue crystal edges. The figure had trouble moving, every effort calculated as though the figure might fall off the side of the mountain at any moment. He looked at his hands inside his white sharp-edged armor, designed to keep his body warm in arctic conditions. It had been so long since he had occupied this body that it took some getting used to. He stumbled as he tried to move, but after dozens of tentative steps, arm swings, and neck turns, he managed to walk again.

"I'm back!" Voice said.

The Air Guardian had followed the coordinates Ratchet had given him and returned to his body. It felt wonderful to be back in his skin and to feel all those old feelings he had forgotten ever since his body was taken from him. For the first time in a long time he remembered how cold it was atop that mountain and what his breath looked like against the freezing temperatures. He cautiously stepped through inches of hard snow, and still he tripped and fell flat on his face in the cold powder. His body was stiff and tense from not being used for so long, but the feeling of the frost and the wind hitting his face was like an old friend coming to say hello. He smiled while lying on the ground; he hadn't felt anything against his skin in so long…and soon he could feel a tear rolling down his cheek. Oh, how Voice loved being back in his body again, feeling truly alive again as a being and a full-bodied guardian.

Voice soon got back up to his feet and regained his balance. He stretched his arms out to feel to icy wind pass between them as he stood proudly atop the frigid mountain, which in a way made him realize how extremely lucky he was that his body had stayed so well preserved, and maybe later he could thank Witch for that. Yes, he was once again the real Voice, the most powerful, respected, and wise being throughout Altered.

Voice closed his blue sparkly eyes, and in a flash he was gone, teleported to a mysterious location high above the sky, with marble arches everywhere, atop an enchanted cloud that was able to secretly hold Cloud Temple high above Altered. This is where the guardians would meet when discussing matters of the utmost importance or seriousness.

Voice entered the center of Cloud Temple and created a blue bubble, which he spoke into. "Attention, Letvia and Inferno. This is a point of emergency. Come to Cloud Temple immediately and with no delays. Or else."

Suddenly the bubble shrank, disappeared, and delivered the message to both Letvia and Inferno, a message that clearly showed Voice was back, powerful, and in a foul mood.

Chapter Ten

Grave Robbers

Before following the coordinates to the Dormancy Catacombs, Gizzy and Benji had decided to go back to Gizzy's shack to take a rest. But when they got to the shack, they found the door wide open and a note on the bed. Figures.

Gizzy picked up the note:

> *Gizzy, I tried to follow you but lost you. I brought you some clothes you may need. The world is big and scary, and you need to stay safe and warm. Also, a heads up; back in the library at the village there is a book about all the creatures that exist in this world. It may be useful for you. See you soon.*
>
> *Brayden*

Gizzy put the note in his pocket and opened up the little red backpack. He took out the magical book with the cute symbol of the fairy on the cover. Gizzy wondered whether or not Benji had done enough to redeem himself or if Gizzy should still de-summon him. Would Benji again lead him into another point of certain danger? Would Gizzy be able to truly trust him from here on out? Had Benji become some sort of friend to him now, or had he only looked out for Gizzy because Gizzy was some kind of master to him and he really had no other choice? So many questions swirled through Gizzy's mind as he held the book.

"Wait, don't do this, please! I've helped you!" Benji pleaded. Going back into the book was the worst form of torture a magic fairy like Benji could suffer. And he was starting to feel Gizzy was becoming a true friend.

"Tell me how you've helped me," Gizzy said.

"I helped you get out of the prison, didn't I? I could have just flown away when Ratchet froze you and picked you up over his shoulder and dragged you back to the castle. I could have left when he threw you behind bars, but I didn't. I stayed behind to make sure you were safe and helped you escape! And look! We're here now. We're safe!"

Benji made some really good points. He could have abandoned Gizzy so many different times, but he stuck by his side. Gizzy was still weighing his options, and Benji could see the uncertainty in his gaze.

"Um, wait! There's more. Don't forget that I showed you Dr. Shamas, who taught you more about your power!"

"Yeah, and have you forgotten that he totally freaked out and tried to kill me? Not to mention that because of you I now also suffer from a split personality, which totally changes everything about my so-called 'power.'"

"No, no! Forget I said that one! Forget that. Um…well, wait a minute. Dr. Shamas said it *might* affect you, but it's not certain. After all, he was infected by a campfire, not a transwolf." Benji gave a huge yawn.

"Um. Campfire? You mean, vampire. Wow, you must be tired."

Benji blinked several times, then fell on the floor of the shack. He rolled around laughing and grabbing his stomach. "Campfire, ha! I said *campfire!*"

"You know, Benji, you're right. Dr. Shamas said *might*, not that it was a certainty I'd end up like him." Maybe Gizzy didn't really have the same kind of sickness that infected Dr. Shamas.

Gizzy closed the book, and Benji sighed with relief.

"I do appreciate the way you stuck by me, Benji. I'm sorry if I've been in a bad mood lately, but being in this new world has been pretty tough on me. I hope you understand."

Gizzy stuck his hand out, and Benji flew up to it and hugged his palm.

Soon after, they left the little shack, walked around the quicksand pool, drank and drank and drank from a nearby stream, ate some herbs and fallen fruits along the way, and had a positive, bright glow about them as the duo followed the coordinates to the graveyard. Just Gizzy and Benji. The Canine and the Fairy. It still had a certain ring to it.

High above the world stood the majestic, stark-white marble structure of Cloud Temple, which provided a beautiful base to watch over the world of Altered. Letvia and Inferno had been summoned by a newly awakened Voice who had an unknown agenda.

Letvia and Inferno were waiting quietly inside the council chamber when Voice arrived. Neither of the guardians had expected to see Voice with his body, and both of them were shocked beyond belief.

"Voice! You got your body back!" Letvia screeched, and she ran up to Voice and gave him a deep and tender embrace. Voice hugged her back weakly, still trying to get used to having his body again. Letvia and Voice had always had a very strong connection, but the bond grew even greater after Elizabeth's passing.

Voice stepped back to admire Letvia. She looked as beautiful as ever with her light blue hair and pale blue skin, ocean-blue eyes, and pink flossy lipstick. Her long dress covered the whole of her sleek body, which was coated in glitter. She had always looked sweet and innocent, though she was responsible for a very powerful element and could manipulate waters in any way she saw fit, changing the levels of the sea, casting water spells, creating rain or sleet or snow.

"It's good to see you again, Voice." Inferno said, not getting up to shake Voice's hand or give him a proper greeting. He was glad to see that Voice was back, but he had never been one to openly express his emotions.

"Same to you," Voice said, looking over Inferno, who was the exact opposite of Letvia. His entire body was made out of lava that was retained by the rocks that made up his body. His eyes were yellow with red pupils, afraid of nothing at all. He was fearless, powerful, demanding. Inferno was the Keeper of the Nether and had gotten very used to trouble. And once Barath was dead and the fire element was passed on to him, there was really little that could stop Inferno if he wanted to raise havoc throughout Altered. And while he had not yet done anything to raise suspicions, Voice felt that he could not be trusted.

"Yes, and as you can see, I'm certainly back. And quite sore, too. And as it turns out, Ratchet knew where my body was this entire time."

"Speaking of Ratchet, where is he?" Letvia asked.

"Causing trouble, probably. I'm really not sure why he's a guardian in the first place," Inferno said.

"Actually...that's why I'm here. He's just too naïve. He does things without thinking. He blackmailed me into luring a complete stranger to Altered into a trap when I was just trying to help the poor boy find his way home. And Ratchet wanted to execute him for treason with little basis for the charge."

"He threatened *you*, Voice!? That's not right! You didn't work this hard to become the most respected being in Altered for some secondary guardian to treat you this way," Letvia said, always very defensive of Voice.

"Thank you, Letvia. I appreciate your sentiment. I wanted to ask your advice about the matter. This stranger...well...he isn't from this world. I was trying to get him to the Prophecy so he could hopefully find his way home. I have a plan, so there's a lot of thought behind my actions, but Ratchet has been causing a lot of problems."

"The Prophecy!? Voice, you know I highly respect you as a guardian, but it's severely dangerous taking a stranger to the Prophecy. I actually see it as a good thing that Ratchet has him captured," Inferno said, clearly irritated and worried.

"Well, actually...the boy escaped."

"What!?" Letvia and Inferno responded in unison. Inferno's anger rose, and Letvia was filled with disappointment.

"Voice, I know you always mean well and that your decisions are often, if not almost always, correct, but this is too much of a threat, and I highly question your judgment on this matter."

"Just hang on," Voice said, wanting to reason with them. "The boy can't get to the Prophecy or have any effect on it without the four keys, so we're safe in that regard. Two of those keys are buried, one is locked away in my kingdom, and the other is, well…is *me*, my aura." Though Voice was laying out a pretty good defense, he was also struggling to keep his composure and remain seemingly neutral in his expressions. Being inside his body again felt like a new experience, and he was worried he wouldn't be able to conceal his secrets.

Letvia stroked her chin, contemplating what Voice had said. "So, taking him to the Prophecy without it being opened with the four keys may actually send him home and hopefully not offer any adverse effects…interesting…although, it's just a theory and only good if it actually works. What I don't understand, though, is why you called us here and say you want our advice, but you have already made your decisions and seem to know what you want to do. Why ask us here at all?"

"Because I betrayed him and took him to Ratchet's kingdom. I wouldn't have done it, except Ratchet was blackmailing me with the coordinates to my body. Had I not led the boy there under false pretenses, then Ratchet could have done anything with my body—burned it, buried it, blew

140

it to pieces. I really had no choice. Before being too harsh with judgments, please consider what the two of you might have done in that circumstance. I had been without a body for too long, and I was so anxious and empty. Anyhow. Now the boy doesn't trust me, and it will take some effort to earn his trust back. And so now, what if he tries to find the four keys and open the Prophecy on his own? What should we do in this instance?"

"He's an alien threat and needs to be found, contained, and dealt with by any means necessary," Inferno quickly said. "And as long as nobody mentions the four keys to him, he shouldn't be able to open the Prophecy anyway." Inferno's eyes were fiery, and he was certain of his position.

"We should at least hear him out!" Letvia said.

"Letvia, maybe you could go down to him and feel out the situation for yourself?" Voice suggested.

"I'd be happy to. I'll go and meet with him and see if he's really going to the Prophecy or if he's decided to abandon the idea for other pursuits. Of course, if he's trying to go on his own and not in the company of a guardian, then it's certain treason, unfortunately. I'm assuming he feels very betrayed by you, Voice, and who knows what that could lead to? Anyhow, I'll report back when I know something so we can all make a final decision together."

Inferno's grimace never left his face, but in the end, he begrudgingly agreed to the plan, and it was settled. Letvia would seek out Gizzy, earn his trust, and hopefully find out his next move.

Meanwhile, back on the solid ground of Altered, Gizzy and Benji had arrived at the Dormancy Catacombs, thanks to the coordinates Gypsy had given them. The creepy graveyard housed thousands upon thousands of old graves. As the brave duo walked down the crooked, eerie pathway between some of the gravestones, the clouds overhead suddenly turned dark and gloomy, echoing the mood of the situation. A chill ran down both of their spines as the realization that they were about to dig up a grave suddenly struck them, and Gizzy wondered how his life had become so strange.

As The Canine and the Fairy walked over, around, and between the graves they noticed something peculiar—there was an empty patch where a gravestone should be. However, as they walked closer, a gravestone suddenly grew out from the ground like a marble flower bursting into life. As the stone finished growing, engraved words spread across its smooth, gray face.

"What just happened?" Gizzy asked.

"A being has just died," Benji said, as he lowered his wings in sadness. Then after a few deep, consoling breaths, he flew over to read the stone and find out who had passed. "Rest in peace, Samantha Telling."

Gizzy slowly looked around the graveyard at the rows and rows of of headstones. It really made him appreciate their next dilemma. "Benji, where do you think we'll find Barath's grave?"

Benji paused, unsure. "I guess we should probably split up; that will be the fastest way and double our chances of finding it."

Benji and Gizzy hugged before they separated, because who really knew what might happen to them in the gloomy graveyard? Though neither of them really wanted to separate, they had agreed that this was probably the quickest way, though not the most comforting.

After a few minutes of scanning the chiseled names and wandering the broken paths, Benji shouted from afar, "Gizzy, if it was a guardian who died, then surely the gravesite or headstone must look different from the rest. Look for one that stands out!" Benji's logic made sense, and Gizzy recalled from Gypsy's lengthy history lesson that both Elizabeth and Barath were dead, and he wondered if they were both buried here.

As they read the gravestones one by one, searching high and low for the one with Barath chiseled on it, Gizzy came across a pretty fresh-looking grave and was shocked to read the name on it... *Betsy the Troll*. Gizzy thought of the little funny troll who had taken the magical book from the library, and here he was, dead. In the ground. No more. The memory of what had happened the night of the chase was very fuzzy for Gizzy. He could recall morphing into the beast and attacking Betsy, but his memory of what had actually happened to Betsy faltered. Whenever he became the wolf, things were always hazy for him, and he figured that was just a side effect of the curse. But after seeing the gravestone and thinking about the vicious attack, he put two and two together and realized...

Oh my god! Gizzy was a murderer!

Even if he was never fully in control of the wolf, he had still technically committed the act. The shock filled Gizzy with a sickness at the bottom of his stomach and an

143

emptiness in his heart. His hands went clammy, and he started to shake uncontrollably. He breathed in deeply through his notes and let the breath out of his mouth. He tried to focus and calm himself. He tried to think of nothing, but the image of poor Betsy kept popping up in his mind.

Gizzy shook his head, trying to discourage his thoughts. Filled with deep guilt and sadness, he wandered the cobbled paths and kept on looking with a half-hearted effort, as he knew he had to press on with their new heavy task. It seemed no quest would ever be truly complete. Sigh. It had never been his intention to harm another being, and he certainly didn't mean to kill Betsy…but then again…he *did*, didn't he? Maybe The Canine had brought out a whole new side of him that he had never seen before…and would never fully see or understand because he could only remember the transformation and actions of the beast in pieces, and really, maybe he was better off that way. Then he thought of what Dr. Shamas had said about his ability…if Gizzy *did* somehow end up with a split personality…would that cause him to kill, too? Would he forever now be part killer beast, part innocent human?

"Gizzy, I found it!" Benji yelled.

Gizzy looked over to see Benji waving his small hands on the other side of the graveyard. Gizzy ran over toward Benji and the grave, weaving in and out of tombstones and trying not to trip over any of the graves. He could see a very large, old crypt with "Here Lies Barath the Barbarian. Remembered as a soldier. Remembered for his duties. Remembered. R.I.P." written above in jagged letters. Purple mossy vines covered the big stone building, and a winding staircase led down into the crypt. There was a lot of dirt piled up around the outside of the crypt, and cobwebs crisscrossed over the entrance, almost forming a kind of foggy door.

Gizzy and Benji worked to wipe away the cobwebs, and after minutes of clearing, their bodies were covered in the gross fibers of the webs. Just before they stepped down the stairs, Gizzy glanced over and saw a very similar tomb only a few hops away. He realized it must have been Elizabeth's crypt, and it almost identically mirrored the design of Barath's. Though, while Barath's crypt was forgotten, neglected, and generally a mess, Elizabeth's was immaculate, polished, and dozens of fresh flowers and flower petals littered the confines of her space. She was obviously adored, and even in her death the beings of Altered wanted to remember her and shed a positive light on her spirit.

"Benji, I can't see anything down there; we're going to need some light," Gizzy said as he made his first steps down the stairs.

"Why didn't you say so sooner?" Benji closed his eyes, balled his fists, and suddenly his whole body was glowing. Apparently he was also a light source!

"Wow! I'm super glad I didn't de-summon you, buddy," Gizzy said, and laughed as he walked down into the crypt below, Benji flying just over his shoulder. They fought cobwebs all along the way as the duo pushed deeper and deeper into the unknown. It was frightening, dark, alone, and eerie, and they began to wonder if this was such a good idea, but they each swallowed the thought and pressed on like good adventurers.

"Benji, I'm going to listen to you this time. If you don't want us to go in and have a better option, then we

145

don't have to do this." Gizzy had been thinking of what had happened last time with Voice, and he was not prepared to take the risk of being betrayed again or putting Benji in a tough position.

"Unfortunately, Gizzy, this time I think we have no other choice...at least if what Gypsy said about needing the four keys to enter the Prophecy is true."

Gizzy was afraid Benji might say that, and he was probably right. If they could just quickly find the Barath Hammer and get out...oh, that would be so awesome!

As they entered the center of the crypt they spotted a tomb in the middle, which most likely held Barath's corpse.

"I'm not trying to point out the obvious here, but the hammer must be in there," Benji whispered.

They walked closer to the tomb to see it was made entirely of stone. It was also covered in disgusting, sticky cobwebs. Tiny spiders owned the floor of the crypt, and Gizzy tried to be careful of where he walked. Benji was fortunate he could fly and easily avoided the mini-monsters. Benji floated over near a corner and came face to face with a giant spider. He was terrified and speechless for a moment as he stared into the five green eyes of the spider and slowly flapped his wings, pushing himself away from the corner.

"Um...Gizzy," Benji squeaked out after coming back to the center of the room. "I don't know about this anymore."

"What do you mean? We've come so far now. All we need is the hammer," Gizzy said, as he began to push the lid of the tomb open. It took all of his strength, but he managed to slowly and surely scoot the top of the tomb until it fell over the edge onto the ground, breaking as it hit the stone floor, sending hundreds of spiders angrily scurrying away. Inside were the remains of Barath, covered in a light shroud. He was an unfortunate being with the great power of fire forced upon him that changed the essence of who he was, creating the mood swings and foul temper that inevitably led to his death. Among the remains lay the Barath Hammer, which had a rusty brown handle with a giant powerful steel top, still strongly gripped by the hand of the skeleton.

Gizzy reached down and lifted the hammer out of the remains and was surprised with how heavy it really was. Gizzy felt a quick sense of strength and relief and a shot of adrenaline at the thought that he was now one step closer to making his way to the Prophecy.

However.

Unbeknown to him, there was a trap rigged inside the crypt, and a loud screeching noise echoed off the cold stone walls. Gizzy reacted by dropping the hammer and covering his ears. The pain of the screech was just too much. He looked over to see the crypt entrance collapsing, the tumbling rubble piling up and sealing them inside.

"If we get locked in here, we're finished!" Benji cried as he flew down toward the ground and tried to help pick up the hammer.

"But I can just turn into an ant and escape like at the jail."

"You can, but the hammer can't!" Benji said, still tugging on the rusted steel.

He was right, if the crypt trapped them inside then they would have to say goodbye to the hammer. But Gizzy was determined not to give up without a fight after everything he had been through. Gizzy hefted the hammer, and the duo headed for the entrance, trying to make it before it was entirely closed. Then suddenly something grabbed Gizzy's ankle, and he fell to the ground. He looked back and noticed it was a lone skeleton hand holding his ankle!

Gizzy kicked and kicked, finally pulling his ankle free of the hand's clutches. Then Gizzy looked up and was completely shocked to see flames burst from the walls and a number of skeletons rise and come alive, glaring at Gizzy as they crept toward him, dragging their skeleton frames. Gizzy was petrified.

Then, the skeleton of Barath sat up inside the exposed coffin, and the bare skull turned and stared at Gizzy. "You will *never* escape Altered!" the skeleton of Barath said.

"Hurry, hurry!" Benji called, hovering near the exit.

Gizzy got to his feet and tried to make his way through the crypt and up the stone staircase as dust fell from the ceiling and rocks and flames poured from the walls. As he was about to jump through the exit the last remaining stone fell, blocking them inside the crypt. The army of skeletons slowly walked toward Gizzy and Benji. Gizzy gripped the Barath Hammer firmly in his hands and began to panic, fearing there was no possible way out of the dreaded crypt. It was beginning to look like the end had finally arrived.

"We're trapped!" Gizzy tried to ram his shoulder into the stones blocking their escape, but the rocks wouldn't budge. "What do we do now!?"

"One will live…and one will die…Altered Earth…" Barath was slowly moving up the stairs with an army of glowing skeletons behind him.

"Earth? Did he say Earth!?" Gizzy asked, confused. It appeared that Barath knew something he didn't.

"Who cares what he said! We need to get out of here," Benji said.

Barath reached out his bony arms as he made his way up the staircase. His skeleton army marched behind him and copied his movements, and now dozens of bony arms were reaching out for the duo. Barath was even so close now that he could nearly grab Gizzy, who was braced against the rubble. As Barath's remaining bony hand reached out, Gizzy remembered the hammer, lifted it with all his might, and swung it as hard as he could, shattering Barath's creepy skeleton with a blast of blue light that sent his bones spraying through the other skeletons, destroying them and clattering hundreds of bones across the floor of the crypt. Though Barath's skeleton was now destroyed, their troubles still weren't over.

Suddenly a loud bang rang out, and Gizzy fell to the ground, knocked forward by an explosion at the exit of the crypt; it felt like a bomb had been detonated, and was that Clayton's laugh coming from outside the crypt, or was Gizzy just hearing things?

Rubble and dust flew past Gizzy as he closed his eyes and covered his head. Benji, who had been floating nearby, braced himself against the stone wall to avoid the flying debris. Gizzy noticed a gap in the debris, but before he could make a move to dive for it, an errant rock hit him in the temple, and he fell to the ground, out like a light.

Gizzy slowly woke behind some bushes, with the beautiful blue trees of Altered dappled all around, their translucent leaves swaying in the wind. He could see two beings arguing in the middle of a field. Suddenly, Gizzy realized that he was in an alternative dream yet again and was watching Voice and the being in the waistcoat, but this time Gizzy was not watching from inside the point of view of Aurona, the child. Gizzy could see dry red skin on a scaly forearm, and he knew he was inside Ratchet's point of view.

"Aurona? Aurona!?" The one in the waistcoat shouted for the child who had accompanied them on the boat, but he received no response. "My brother! My brother was on that boat, and now he's gone! This is your damn fault, Voice!"

"For the most part, the plan went exactly how it was supposed to go! I'm sorry about your brother, but Gizzy's now in Altered. Isn't that what we were trying to accomplish? Look, I really am sorry about Aurona, but I know we'll find him. I apologize, but I need to go meet Gizzy before he wanders off."

Voice turned to walk away, but the being in the waistcoat aggressively grabbed his arm.

"I don't care about that right now! Where in the hell's my brother, Voice!?" His voice was filled with anger. Clearly he had conspired with Voice to get Gizzy on the cruise ship and have him teleported to Altered by using Aurona's powers and the creation of the cyclone, but Aurona was never meant to actually follow them to Earth, and now the young child had gone missing.

"I already said that I don't know where Aurona is, and I'm sorry! But the plan went forward and seems to have been a success. I need to go and find Gizzy if we want him to save our world!"

"And how successful was the plan, really, when you've lost my ten-year-old brother? Not to mention the huge pirate ship that docked beside the cruise ship and the pirates who boarded in a crude attempt to overtake it."

"Look, we can find the pirates and get rid of them. It shouldn't be a big problem. How far could they really get? And I'm sure I saw your brother enter the cyclone to come back to Altered with us, and even if not, he has such strong powers that he can just make a new cyclone and come back in that one."

"My priority lies with my brother. Do what you want with Gizzy, I'm going to find Aurona before he ends up dead, if he isn't already!"

"Fine! And I care about finding your brother, too, but dammit, saving this beautiful world of ours takes precedence, and whether you like it or not, the truth is that it's far more important than your brother or any other singular being!"

The one in the waistcoat looked at Voice in shock after what he had just said.

"I used to have a ton of respect for you, but you've become so absorbed with the egotistical notion of saving Altered that you've lost sight of what really matters. And now you're going to pay for those words."

The being with the long waistcoat pressed his hands together and created a strange blue light from his palms.

Then he violently pushed the light toward Voice as he slowly chanted, causing Voice's body to slowly disappear. After all this time, Gizzy suddenly realized who this figure was—it was Witch!

"Sissem, Magicka Soulessa," Witch said, and suddenly there was a great flash, and Voice's body was gone. Witch looked around for Voice, and Ratchet ducked even lower behind the bushes to stay out of sight.

"What the hell did you do!?" Voice asked, now nothing more than a kind of consciousness.

Gizzy still didn't understand how he was integral to saving this planet he had never been to and didn't even know existed until a handful of days ago. How was he so important to all this, and why was Gizzy the one who was chosen to save this world?

"I removed your body with a spell I've been working on for quite some time now. Maybe if you had chosen your words a little more carefully this wouldn't have happened. But you've started to become careless and arrogant, and if you want to remain the most respect being in all of Altered, then maybe this will give you something to think about and cause you to rethink the way you treat others and where your priorities lie. I'm not perfect, but I can still see when another being has gone too far, and this...*this*, Voice, is a fitting punishment for such a ridiculous name."

Suddenly, Ratchet raised himself up from the bushes and ran over toward where Witch was standing.

"Ah, there you are, Ratchet," Witch said. He had a very confident look on his face, like he had absorbed a mass of power.

"So glad to see your mighty spell worked, sir!" Ratchet said. Gizzy was surprised that he could understand Ratchet in the dream, considering he didn't speak Greenbloodian. But then he figured he was probably able to understand the words because he was within Ratchet and seeing and feeling everything from his perspective. This made Gizzy wonder about the dreams themselves. Why was it so important for him to have these dreams and to know about what had happened before he had arrived in Altered? It felt like there were always too many questions and not enough answers; however, these different perspectives really did help to reveal a lot of secrets to him. It was also strangely fortunate that he had knocked himself out so many times.

"You monster!" Voice said. Just from the sound of his voice, it was clear he was in agony from having been separated from his body.

Witch laughed. Then he pointed to the sky and taunted poor Voice.

In retaliation, Voice sent down a bright light that struck Witch, and he fell to the ground. Then he sent another bolt down and hit Ratchet, who also fell to the ground.

Witch quickly got to his feet and yelled into the sky, "Good luck ever getting your body back!"

"We'll see who has worse luck, Witch. I'm calling a meeting with the other guardians, and let's see who they side with when they find out you've betrayed the most honored and respected being in all of Altered. You may think you've got the upper hand now, but I'd be willing to guarantee that after hearing news like that, within no time you'll be stripped of your guardianship and be back to nothing more than a

153

regular Power-Born. And don't come crying to me when it does happen, just remember that you messed with the wrong guardian."

"Ha! Think again, Voice. They wouldn't dare to vote against me and strip me of my power. Not in a million years."

Silence.

"I said, not in a million years! You hear me, Voice!?"

Gizzy woke up from his dream. Benji was lightly slapping him on the face and had an incredibly worried look. Gizzy blinked several times.

"Get up, get up, get up!" Benji said, tugging on Gizzy's jacket. "Follow me, and grab the hammer."

Gizzy got up, barely able to lift the hammer, and followed Benji through the small hole in the rubble. When they got outside the crypt, Gizzy dropped the hammer and laid down in the grass. His head was thumping so hard.

"What just happened?" Gizzy asked. "I feel like I have a migraine."

"The tomb collapsed, and a rock hit your big dumb head and knocked you out. I was worried sick!" Benji crossed his arms in front of his chest and dropped his wings.

"How do I keep managing to get knocked out? Maybe it's my only true super power," Gizzy joked. "Ah, my head!"

Benji cracked a smile. "Well, stop making a habit of it, darn you! I hate worrying!"

"At least we're safe now, my friend," Gizzy said, as he picked himself up off the ground, his head spinning. He took several deep breaths, then took off his little red backpack. He unzipped the bag, grabbed the Barath Hammer, and set it inside. When he put the backpack on his back again, Gizzy walked to and fro, getting used to lugging the weapon around.

"Hey, Wandering Boy, the clock's ticking, ya know! We should really get moving," Benji said.

It was clear they needed to find shelter soon or they would probably end up as food for some unknown Altered beast.

"Just trying to get a feel for the hammer. Anyway, I say we go back to the village and find Brayden. I think that's the logical next step."

Benji nodded, and they started heading in the direction of Cobblebury, Gizzy walking and Benji flying just beside his shoulder as had become ritual for them. It would be a fairly long journey and would take several hours to get back to the tiny village. Along the way, Gizzy couldn't help thinking about what had happened since he had arrived in Altered and also what had happened or was happening now that he didn't even know about. He was certain that Voice and Witch had planned the cyclone and that he was apparently here to save Altered, but he still couldn't figure out why or who in the heck or what in the heck he was supposed to be saving it from.

Forty feet underground, in the Lucky Ore Cavern, Gypsy was lying on one of his infamous rugs, having a long rest and still thinking about the meeting he had had with Gizzy and Benji. He was happy that he could offer them a brief safe haven from the guardians.

Suddenly, the light from the fire was blocked, and the glow of the room lessened. Gypsy opened his eyes and saw a figure standing in front of him, drowning out most of the light from the fire.

"Well, did you find him!?" Gypsy asked, unsteady and eager for an answer.

Witch didn't respond and instead looked away, ashamed.

Gypsy quickly stood, walked up to Witch, and slapped him across the face.

"Find my son! You go and find him if it's the last thing you do! Please, dammit! Please." Gypsy grabbed Witch by the back of the neck and pulled him into an intense embrace. They cried against each other's shoulders, so sad and desperate without the youngest of their clan.

"Please, know that I'm trying, Father! I'm really trying, and I'm sorry I haven't been able to find him." Witch had always strived to earn his father's love, but Gypsy was a tough Power-Born who often didn't show support or give love. Their embrace was a rare thing, and Witch cherished the moment, until his father let go and stepped away. Witch often got the cold shoulder from Gypsy. He was always considered the distant sibling because he was older than Aurona and was often away learning new voodoo spells and trying to capture the essence of the practice. It was especially hard for Witch after his mother had passed away many years earlier, and since Aurona was only ten years old now and had greater special powers, he earned the most attention, and that had left Witch far behind and full of deep sadness.

"I spoke with Gizzy, and he said he's heading to the Prophecy. He's going to gather the four keys and hopefully open the Prophecy. Everything seems to be falling into place."

Witch wiped the tears from his face and flashed a brief smile. "That's great news, Father. Ever since I lost my position as the Earth Guardian, my life has been a total mess. You're stuck hiding here, and Aurona's gone missing. I want revenge on all the guardians for siding with Voice and voting to kick me out. Not to mention that Voice's ridiculous plan had to involve Aurona, and it's his fault my little brother has gone missing. They've ruined my life and turned me into a social outcast. It can never go back to the way it was, but we can strive to make it better! If we can ensure that Gizzy opens the Prophecy, I can become the ruler of the whole planet. No Guardians this time, only me…and I will be king!"

Gypsy had a look of uncertainty on his face. "Remember that I can see into the future. You will become the king of Altered, but in order to do so you must help Gizzy. Become his friend and help him get the four keys to the Prophecy. He should already have the hammer by now, but you…did you hear something?"

Gypsy stopped talking and looked around. Witch looked around, too.

"I didn't hear anything," Witch said. "These caverns are full of sweeple mice and closet bats. Maybe they're migrating through the tunnels."

"You're right. It was probably nothing, sorry. But what I was saying is that you need to find a way to get into Voice's kingdom and get your shield back. If he hadn't taken it off you when you were exiled, this would be a much easier task."

"I couldn't help it, Father, they voted me out, and he demanded my shield. It was three against one. But I promise to find a way. And…thank you for helping me."

Witch turned and was about to leave the cavern, when Gypsy tugged on his arm.

"One more thing that I think you must know…my visions see Alpha, but he's…he's alive."

Witch shrugged his father's hand off him and turned angry, as if the name of Alpha haunted him and everything he had been fighting for.

"Alpha's alive!? But that's impossible! I saw him die! I was there!"

"Correct. He's dead now, but my visions show him as being alive in the future. If you want to be the king of Altered, you *must* follow my visions in order for the future to happen the way we want it to. My visions are not perfect, but they are almost always correct. Believe in that, and believe in them."

"But, Father, only the Chosen One can bring him back from the dead! We don't know where Alpha's son is or even *who* he is!"

"Fear not, my son. I believe that the Chosen One is in fact *not* the prince of Altered. Whoever he is."

Witch's eyes glistened when he heard this. There was still hope to bring the king back from the dead.

"I believe that Gizzy is the Chosen One, brought here to raise King Alpha from the dead. He must be the one foreseen to save us, and he has come from another world, after all. He is most likely the one to bring Alpha back to life. Who else could it be? And if he does this, the future will follow as it should…still giving you a fair chance to be king."

"But, what if Alpha gets in the way of that goal?"

"You'll find a way. Remember my vision where *you* become king. Whether Alpha is alive or not. Take solace in that notion, and go find my son. Aurona's out there somewhere. I can feel it."

"Don't worry, Father. I will."

Witch left the cavern to finish his quest for revenge. Voice had removed two very important things from his life—his seat as Earth Guardian and his brother. Filled with guilt, shame, and anger, Witch was willing to go as far as he possibly could to get everything back. He realized he needed to find Gizzy and tell him to free the king so the future could move forward as planned.

"That's my boy!" Gypsy wished his son good luck on his quest to become the king of Altered. He was also furious with the guardians for exiling Witch, and he was especially angry with Voice for coming up with the ridiculous plan that vanished his youngest boy. Now that both of his sons were essentially taken from him, Gypsy also had a thirst for revenge and would do whatever it took to help Witch achieve his goals. It was fortunate he could see into the future, but there were gray spots in the visions, things he couldn't fully see or only saw in flashes.   As Witch exited the cavern and took off across the hard land of Altered in search of Gizzy, he was unaware that he was being watched by Ratchet, who had hidden just outside the exit, which he had found by following Gizzy's scent, not to mention the fact that he had done a lousy job covering the exit hole.

Ratchet was outside wringing his hands. He needed to find Clayton before he took on Gypsy. Confronting a being who could see into the future would be a tough task by himself. Ratchet walked away with a big smile on his face—he had heard everything.

Chapter Eleven

The Last Warning

As they moved closer to Cobblebury, Gizzy could sense something was horribly wrong. He could smell ash and smoke. Odd, because he had never sensed a smell so strongly before, so this had to be bad. Even Benji, who was now cowering behind Gizzy, knew something was wrong as they crept closer to the village. Gizzy, acting only on instincts, took off sprinting, and Benji beat his wings quickly behind him.

When they reached the village, tired and out of breath, they found it…well…gone. All that remained of the historic, peaceful village was ash and the smell of decay. Not a single Nose People Character was in sight, and Gizzy felt a sharp pain in his heart. Gizzy ran through the ashes, kicking them and sweeping through them with his hands, desperately trying to find someone, trying to find even a speck of life.

"Gizzy, it's not safe here!" Benji tried to pull Gizzy back with his tiny fairy hands, but Gizzy kept pushing forward, hoping that someone would emerge from the grayness and the awful smell of death.

Soon they arrived at a collapsed, burned-out building, and Gizzy recognized it as the shop where Brayden had lived. Gizzy's heart sank even more, and he felt so sick that he thought he might throw up.

"Gizzy, it's just not safe here. I'm really sorry to say this, but it's clear nobody…survived. We should leave now before something bad happens to us, too!"

Gizzy, still in shock, nodded and followed Benji out of the rubble and into a nearby forest, where even the surrounding nature seemed sadly silent.

Suddenly, a figure appeared up ahead beside a tree.

"Someone survived!" Gizzy shouted to get the stranger's attention. "Hey! Over here!"

"No, no!" Benji quickly covered Gizzy's mouth. "That doesn't look like an NPC to me. That being's probably dangerous!"

The figure stepped away from the blue tree and started walking toward them. Not only did it not look like an NPC but, much to Gizzy's horror, it was a familiar face from his past...the reason he was in this mess in the first place...

"Gizzy!?" Clayton said, holding explosives in his hands, ready to flip the switch.

"Clayton!?" Gizzy was completely horrified when he saw Clayton with the explosive devices and couldn't comprehend how his old best friend had changed so drastically in such a short period of time. Gizzy really didn't know what Clayton was capable of anymore after seeing the carnage and utter devastation he had caused.

A terrified Benji flew down into some bushes, barely able to watch through the leaves as Clayton stepped closer to Gizzy, causing Gizzy to hesitantly move backward. Clayton walked Gizzy down, dropped the explosives, and grabbed Gizzy by the collar of his gray jacket. Clayton's eyes were bloodshot and full of darkness. The innocent teenage boy Gizzy had known most of his life was entirely gone, erased forever, and only the shell of Clayton remained.

"I thought I'd taken care of you back at the crypt," Clayton said.

"So it *was* a bomb that exploded near the exit!" Gizzy said, exasperated.

"Oh, so it was," Clayton said in a coy manner.

Clayton was too close for comfort, but Gizzy was pinned against the tree and also fearful of what Clayton might do next after having just destroyed an entire village, murdering dozens of innocent Nose People Characters, and apparently he had tried to kill Gizzy, too, or at least trap him in the old crypt.

"How…how could you do this?" Gizzy asked, still shocked that Clayton was so willing to commit murder.

"It was all because of you, really." Clayton's words haunted Gizzy. "Everybody here is dead because of you."

"Me? But, why!?"

"Because you're going to the Prophecy! My master told me to do whatever was necessary to stop you…and I obeyed his command." Clayton let go of Gizzy's jacket, and Gizzy edged away from the tree trunk.

Unbeknown to the dueling Earthlings, someone was watching them from a good distance away…Letvia. As she had promised Voice and Inferno, she had found Gizzy and was watching over him to find out whether or not he was truly going to the Prophecy, but instead she had also uncovered the shocking horror of the massacred village and had now just found out that Clayton's master, Ratchet, had given him the authority to destroy it.

"Why does your master not want me to go to the Prophecy…Cib?" Gizzy used the old nickname in the hopes that hearing it might bring some sense back to Clayton and spark the good inside, if there was any left.

The angry pirate hesitated at the name and briefly remembered some of the good times they'd had together when they were growing up…but something was holding him back, an evil anger from deep within and the loyalty to his new master.

"The Prophecy will take us home, Cib. We could go back to Earth together and start over!"

Clayton's eyes lit up for a moment, glimmering for a brief second, before the darkness took over again. "You're a liar!" Clayton viciously struck Gizzy to the ground and picked up the explosives. Then he stepped back to a safe distance with Gizzy still on the ground. Clayton clutched the hazardous devices, ready to blow everything apart. "Ratchet told me to get rid of you…and I must do what he commanded. Goodbye, old friend; you know where I'll see you again." Clayton was about to detonate the explosives as Gizzy lay helpless on the ground. He knew he wouldn't be able to outrun the explosion, and maybe this was somehow a perfect way to go after everything that had happened to him…killed by someone he had loved and adored like a brother.

"Gizzy! Close your eyes, now!" A familiar voice had emerged from the rubble, and Gizzy immediately shut his eyes. Suddenly there was bright flash that blinded Clayton, and he dropped the explosives to cover his face. "Gizzy, run!" the voice said, and Gizzy got up and took off with Benji in hot pursuit, flapping his wings like a maniac fairy.

As Gizzy and Benji escaped the destroyed village and Clayton's clutches, the blinding light slowly dissipated. In the distance, Gizzy could hear Clayton shouting after Gizzy, but Clayton couldn't see a thing.

Just as Gizzy and Benji had made their getaway and were finally in the clear, they ran into a familiar face…

"Brayden!? What did you—"

"I'll explain later, let's just get the heck out of here! To the shack!" Brayden said, and he grabbed Gizzy's arm, urging him to run.

When all three of them had made it back to the shack and had some time to breathe and calm down, Brayden delivered some startling news. "I have an ability. I'm a Power-Born."

"So that explains why you look different from everyone else," Benji said.

"Yes, and I don't know why or how I was given the ability, but I recently discovered it. I'm able to create a ball of light so bright that it's able to temporarily blind other beings."

"Have you met anyone else like you?" Benji asked Brayden.

"No, never."

Gizzy had been silent the whole time, and Benji and Brayden both looked at him. He was clearly in shock, still in his own world inside his mind, thinking and wondering. One thought haunted him more than any other: Cib was a murderer.

"Wake up, you fool!" Ratchet said, nudging Clayton from his sleep. Clayton had fallen to the ground unconscious after being blinded by Brayden's bright light.

"What happened?" Clayton asked, blinking his eyes. He was thankful that he was able to see again. He got to his feet and faced Ratchet, who had fire in his eyes.

"Did you cause this destruction!?" Ratchet asked, looking around at the demolished buildings, the piles of ash, and the scattered corpses of many Nose People Characters.

"Yes, I did. I did it for you! You told me to stop Gizzy from going to the Prophecy, and it was clear that people in this village were harboring him, aiding him, and even some of the security forces were in on the plan to get Gizzy to the Prophecy. What was I supposed to do? Let them help him to a sacred place that might destroy our entire planet? They needed to be stopped!"

"Clayton, you idiot!" Ratchet had deeply liked Clayton and had tried his best to care for him and mend him, but he was beyond angry with Clayton's ill-conceived actions. "Don't you understand how much trouble you've made for us now?"

Before another word, a bright blue light came down from the sky, quickly encircled them, and the duo was suddenly teleported away by the glowing orb. Suddenly they were inside Cloud Temple, along with Voice, Inferno, and Letvia, who were waiting for them, looks of anger and contempt on their faces.

"Oh no," Ratchet said, knowing very well that this was an immediate trial about what Clayton had done. One of the guardians must have somehow found out, and they were both unaware that Letvia had seen the aftermath of the destruction of the village with Clayton taking responsibility, then assaulting Gizzy. Ratchet was deathly afraid. He knew that this would probably be the moment he had been dreading, when he would be dethroned as the Earth Guardian.

"Hello, my fellow guardians. Good to see you again," Ratchet said, trying to make peace.

"Silence!" Inferno shouted, terrifying Ratchet. Inferno's powers were so much mightier than Ratchet's, and Inferno had always been more aggressive toward him, especially whenever Ratchet slipped up.

"Ratchet, you're officially on trial, so please don't speak unless spoken to," Voice said. Voice was almost always the being of utmost reason, and Ratchet felt much safer being spoken to by him. "Ratchet, you're on trial for the murder of the NPCs from the village of Cobblebury. You're also being tried for allowing Gizzy to escape, a human who's a threat to our planet."

"I'm sorry, Voice, but you said Gizzy was only trying to get home and that he wasn't a threat."

"Those were your words, not mine," Voice said.

"But I didn't kill the NPCs, Clayton did! I told him to help protect the Prophecy, and he had evidence that the village of Cobblebury was harboring Gizzy and had plans to help him reach the Prophecy."

167

"That's true!" Clayton said, unafraid to defend himself. But when he saw the evil scowl on Inferno's face, he slowly backed down, knowing he wasn't allowed to speak. Both Ratchet and Clayton were terrified of what might happen.

"What about the deaths of all the innocents?" Voice asked Ratchet. "How will you account for this?"

"If I had known he was going to destroy the entire village, I never would have sent him off to stop Gizzy in the first place. Please, you have to believe me," Ratchet said.

"Or you would have at least mended your speech and clarified your meaning?" Letvia asked.

"Yes, of course!" Ratchet said. "It was just a horrible miscommunication. The boy, he's…he's not been well since I first found him. I've tried and tried to heal him and correct him, but something's missing inside him. So much is broken. There is little I can do."

Clayton stared at nothing at all. It was as if he couldn't comprehend what he had become, but the flowing spirit of the universe understood his horrifying shift and the tragic loss of Cib.

Letvia, Voice, and Inferno formed a tight circle and held a private conference about the matter, attempting to come to a conclusion about how to deal with the issue. Soon, they came to a decision and turned to face the accused.

"Ratchet, it was clear that your instructions to Clayton were heartfelt in your attempt to save the planet from what you thought would be utter destruction if Gizzy reached the Prophecy. Since your intent was just, and quite frankly we have no present suitors to fill your command, you will not be dethroned over this, though you will be under a timeline of suspension, where you may not slip up, act of order, or make even the slightest mistake. You will reduce the use of your powers and contact your fellow guardians in the event of any impactful decision you might make. Is that clear?"

"Oh, thank you, Voice! Thank you, thank you, thank you! It's entirely clear, and I want to praise my fellow guardians for being so just and lenient with me. I'm still learning, after all," Ratchet said, overjoyed with the good news.

"But…" Inferno said, and the others turned around in fear, realizing Inferno was not satisfied as he stood tall and proud and strong. "You still blackmailed Voice into tricking Gizzy to your kingdom and then put him in jail. Not only that, but people are dead because of your incompetence and the actions of your direct subordinate. You weren't clear about what to do and how to do it, and it wasn't his job to protect our wonderful planet…it's ours. You failed in your task, and because of that…innocent NPCs are dead."

"You rang, master?" From behind a pillar stepped a familiar face to Clayton, another boy who was now unexpectedly reunited with his old friend. It was Hugh, the leader of the pirate gang. His entire body was locked in chains, and he was now a slave to Inferno.

Ratchet felt a sense of sadness for the poor boy, who was helpless as Inferno's captive. At least Ratchet had befriended Clayton, mended his wounds, and attempted to heal his mind. Hugh was nothing more than an abused slave, treated as a much lesser being of little to no worth.

"Clayton!" Hugh shouted, then coughed, but covered in chains, he was unable to move toward his old friend.

Inferno shoved Hugh to the ground, then walked toward Clayton. Ratchet instinctively stepped in front of Clayton to protect him.

"Inferno, what are you trying to do here? Your point has been taken," Ratchet said, and then he looked down to see sharp, fiery claws grow out of Inferno's red-hot hands.

"You need to live with the consequences of your choices, and maybe this will teach you a lesson and remind you of what you're dealing with!" Inferno suddenly disappeared in a cloud of smoke. There was silence inside Cloud Temple as everyone looked nervously around. Ratchet circled Clayton, doing his best to shield him. Soon, Ratchet was thrown to the ground, and a blood curdling cry rang out. A razor-sharp claw stabbed through Clayton's body, piercing his young heart.

"Clayton!!!" Ratchet screamed on the top of his lungs as he watched the life of his friend fade away. He hurried himself off the ground, with no way of saving his friend. It was too late.

Inferno pulled his claw out, and Clayton's body dropped, dead before he even hit the ground. Hugh screamed for his old friend. Ratchet clasped Clayton's bleeding body.

"Clayton! Everything will be okay!" Ratchet yelled, holding the body in the hope that he could give comfort in some way, but it was too late. Ratchet closed his eyes and put his last few remaining explosive devices in his pockets. Then he rose with tears streaming down his face. He was devastated at the loss of his companion and for the utter mistakes he had made.

Inferno violently grabbed Ratchet by the neck and picked him up off the ground, squeezing until Ratchet was unable to breathe. *"That* was your last warning." He then threw Ratchet to the ground, and Ratchet choked and gasped for air. "Now, get out of my sight!"

Ratchet fled, but just before he left Cloud Temple, he took one last look at Clayton's limp body. "Goodbye, dear friend," he whispered. "I tried. I really did." Then, Ratchet was gone.

"Inferno, you beast! Why did you do that? This wasn't supposed to be part of the trial!" Voice said, as Inferno stood over Clayton's body.

"Because Ratchet needed to be punished for his incompetence and hopefully learn something for once."

"Inferno, you know death at the hand of a guardian means the soul will be gone forever and can never come back!" Letvia said, angry with Inferno's actions. She went over to comfort Hugh, who was in tears.

"I know," Inferno carefully spoke. Then he lifted his hands over Clayton's body, and suddenly the dead boy was in flames. Soon the body would turn to ash and soon be gone, but never forgotten.

Chapter Twelve:

Higher Rank

Gizzy and Benji continued to follow Brayden into the unknown. They left the shack having drank lots of water, gathered food, and taken a few moments to breathe and try to absorb it all. But they felt they had no time to sit around and wait, so they took off following Brayden's lead.

"Can you please just tell me where we're going?" Gizzy asked. "I'm tired of asking by now."

Brayden still didn't answer, and they kept walking.

Gizzy looked at Benji, who was now flying by his side, and the look on Benji's face made it seem like he probably knew where they were headed. Gizzy decided to try a new tactic and stopped walking. "I'm not walking any farther until you explain where we're going!"

"Fine. We're going to Higher Rank!" Brayden said.

"Hello!? Higher Rank? Unless you've both forgotten, I'm not from here and have no idea what Higher Rank is. Can one of you please explain it to me?"

"Higher Rank is a village that hosts the community called the Rebellion. The Rebellion is a cult against the guardians. A lot of people don't believe that the guardians should be ruling the planet and that the true king lies underground."

Gizzy gave in and started walking again, somewhat satisfied.

"So…we're going there to help them stop the guardians from continuing to rule the planet?"

"Yes!" Benji said, as the trio entered the forest.

As they got closer and closer to Higher Rank, Gizzy could almost feel a sense of something like satisfaction or a little bit of hope inside. After everything that had happened on this adventure, he found himself once again thinking about home, wondering about the well-being of his mother, and whether or not he would ever be reunited with her…or if he even wanted to be.

"I almost forgot, here you go!" Brayden took off his tatty yellow backpack and handed it over to Gizzy. "Open it up."

Gizzy opened the backpack and found a small red book inside: *The Good, the Bad, and the Just Plain No-No: The Magical Book of Mystical Creatures.* "I think this will really come in handy for you, and at the very least it should educate you some more about our planet and what lives here."

"Thanks!" Gizzy reached for the book, but Benji was faster and took it away, laughing.

"I want to read it!" Benji said, and he flipped open the book to a random page. "Hey, look, I'm in here!" Benji pointed to a similar-looking fairy as Brayden and Gizzy looked on with interest.

The Colossal Fairy. Only obtained through a very specific set of enchanted books. This fairy has the power of healing cursed victims but may leave the nasty scar of a split personality. If killed, the fairy can be resummoned using the same enchanted book by which the fairy was released, but if that particular book is destroyed, then the fairy will be lost forever.

"Interesting!" Gizzy said, and the trio continued walking.

"Does it say anything about the split personality?" Gizzy asked Benji, who looked funny holding the disproportionately large book. But as long as Benji used the strength of his beating wings, he could carry much heavier objects. He flicked through some pages to see if he could find anything more about the split personality, but there was nothing.

"Hey, check this out," Benji said. "The bludder shark is one of the more intellectually superior beings in Altered, with the ability to speak any language fluently. If bitten by a bludder shark, a surviving victim will henceforth be able to understand every language spoken in Altered."

"Wait, what does that mean, exactly?" Gizzy asked, confused.

"It means if you get bitten by a bludder shark and survive to tell the tale, then you can understand *everyone* in Altered."

"So if I ever wanted to understand Ratchet and communicate with him in Greenbloodian, that would mean I would need to be bitten by a bludder shark!?" Gizzy laughed, then hesitated at the thought.

Benji dropped the book and fell to the ground, doing his obnoxious laugh. Gizzy felt a little embarrassed that Brayden had to witness this over-the-top display, but Brayden didn't seem to mind the ridiculous fairy, and he was actually quite fond of the little guy and felt he was a good companion. The trio seemed to fit well together, and Brayden had promised Gizzy that Higher Rank was a truly safe haven in Altered. A place where the beings would take care of Gizzy and Benji and help them to the Prophecy.

"Let's get moving again," Brayden said, waving the other two along.

Benji was about to pick the book up off the ground, when he read over the opened page. Soon Benji had a fearful look on his face like he had just seen a ghost.

"Benji, what's wrong?" Gizzy asked. Then he walked over and stared down at the page Benji was on, ninety-two.

The Green Bloods. Once used to rule the land, now close to extinction. Their pale red skin was at one point the most valued resource in all of Altered. Hunting teams would track them and skin them alive. The most famous of these hunters were known as the Bowsmen and had hunted the Green Bloods to near extinction. Only a few Green Blood remain.

Benji wasn't afraid of the article, but he was nervous about what was written at the bottom of the page…the word *LUCK* was written in blood, staining the page with deep-red lettering.

"Luck?" Brayden had never seen anything so peculiar, but Benji was frightened because he and Gizzy had seen this before.

"That was written on the wall inside Ratchet's kingdom," Gizzy said.

"It was also written in blood," Benji said, shocking Brayden. "This was deliberately written into the book, and whoever wrote it also purposefully singled out the page about the Green Bloods…and Ratchet is a Green Blood."

"Let's not forget about the Lucky Ore Cavern," Gizzy said.

Benji nodded. He was shaking with fear.

"Brayden, where did you get this book?" Gizzy asked.

Before Brayden could answer, Gizzy suddenly felt frozen again. "Wait, something's wrong with me," Gizzy said. "I can't move."

"Gizzy? What's going on?" Brayden asked.

"I…I can't move, either!" Benji said. He and Gizzy were stuck to where they were standing, and suddenly a blue orb surrounded them, growing brighter and brighter.

"You're being teleported by a guardian. No!" Brayden said, and he tried to grab Gizzy, but he was too slow. Gizzy and Benji disappeared, leaving Brayden alone…again.

Gizzy looked up, now no longer in the forest but in the middle of an ocean. It seemed clear, and for a second, he wondered if he had been teleported back to Earth and had landed where the cruise ship had been destroyed by the cyclone. But when he turned around he saw a giant ice kingdom floating in the middle of the ocean. Gizzy was definitely still in Altered. He was happy to see Benji was still with him, at least, and the two friends walked up to the ice kingdom together.

"Here, you should take this back," Benji said, handing the red book over to Gizzy who put it inside his little red backpack. They walked into the tall kingdom made of long pillars and sapphire, and Benji immediately knew where they were.

"This was Elizabeth's castle before she died," Benji said. "She was Letvia's sister and the first Water Guardian. You might remember that she tragically died a while ago."

Gizzy nodded, and they walked deeper into the bright blue kingdom to find Letvia standing in the center. Letvia was the most beautiful woman Gizzy had ever seen.

"Gizzy, it's so good to finally meet you. My name is Letvia, and I'm the Water Guardian." Gizzy had now met three out of the four guardians, Inferno being the only one missing from the list.

"It's nice to meet you, too, Letvia. Why did you bring us here? You're not trying to capture me, are you?"

Letvia laughed softly. "I was informed by Voice and Ratchet that you might be going to the Prophecy, so I teleported you here, far away from any threat or danger. I wanted to ask you myself. Instead of locking you away or blackmailing you or lying to you, I will ask you directly." Letvia was kind and sweet; she knew what to say to make Gizzy feel safe. "I know it must be very hard with your friend being dead, and your heart is probably swelling with anger, but the guardians are here to help you."

"Wait… *dead*? Who's dead?"

Letvia realized that Gizzy didn't know about Clayton's grizzly end…how could he?

177

"Oh, my goodness. I didn't mean to let that slip. I'm so sorry, Gizzy, but there was a trial to determine what would happen with your friend, Clayton, because of what he had done to the innocent villagers, and Inferno, the Fire Guardian...well...he killed him..."

Gizzy paused. He didn't know how to feel or how he was supposed to react. Cib, the true friend he had known for most of life had been gone for a while, and now Clayton, the shell of Cib, was dead.

"I...I really don't know what to say. I just hope you understand that the Clayton you knew from this planet was not the same Clayton that I knew back home on Earth. He was known as Cib back home, and Cib was the best kind of person anybody would hope to meet, and I hope he will be remembered that way."

"Fair enough," Letvia said. "And again, I'm very sorry for the loss."

"Thank you," Gizzy said, and then he nodded, as if he was ready for her to move forward with whatever she had to say.

"So, what I wanted to ask you was...are you truly going to the Prophecy?"

"No," Gizzy lied. "At this point, I'm just exploring Altered and all the beauty it has to offer. I was told that the Prophecy is only a myth, and I'm glad to leave it at that."

Letvia gave a faint smile, then nodded.

Soon a blue orb surrounded the duo again, and Gizzy and Benji were quickly teleported back to where they had come from. They looked around for Brayden, but he was nowhere in sight. Gizzy, however, stumbled upon a compass that had been left on the ground with coordinates inside. That Brayden, always thinking ahead! Gizzy picked up the compass and started moving in the direction of Higher Rank.

"Hey!" Benji said, flying up to Gizzy. "Why did you lie to her about the Prophecy?"

"I was locked up by Ratchet when he thought I was going to the Prophecy, and I was betrayed by Voice. We were in the middle of nowhere, and she could have easily killed us and dumped our bodies in the water…plus, the guardians killed Clayton. I owe it to Cib to either get home or save this planet, otherwise his death was in vain."

Brayden finally made it to Higher Rank, a big village with giant towers that were guarded all day and night. In the center of the village was a great Victorian-style castle surrounded by quaint red-and-yellow cottages. Different shops made of stone were sprinkled about, and small farms lined the outskirts of town. As the name suggested, the Rebellion was full of rebellious Nose People Characters and Justments who despised the idea that the guardians were now ruling the world. They all belonged to a movement that followed the values of the long-lost king and had built and implemented a training camp for soldiers who would one day lead a revolt against the guardians.

Brayden walked up to a guard wearing full blue armor and a steel helmet. "Take me to Commander Tayren. I've found the Chosen One." As soon as he said this, the beings around him gasped, including the guard, who promptly escorted Brayden to the most beautiful-looking home inside Higher Rank, which was a rather idyllic community that saw no hunger, no homelessness, and no violence. Every time somebody signed up for the Rebellion they were given a job as a cook, a guard, a farmer, a nurse, a servant, etc.

They stepped up to the beautiful house, and the guard knocked on the door. Soon the door opened, and the guard stepped aside so Brayden could walk inside…alone. Brayden walked into the home to find an elderly being sitting at a desk with his back to Brayden—it must be the great Tayren!

"Welcome. I heard you have some news for me," Tayren said, and then he turned to face Brayden, revealing a giant scar down the right side of his face.

"Ye-Yes sir!" Brayden stammered, surprised to see the rough scar. "I've found the Chosen One! His name is Gizzy, and he came here from a distant planet called Earth."

Tayren laughed, then walked over and hugged Brayden. "Finally! I'm so happy to hear this news. We've been waiting for the Chosen One who will save us from the grips of the guardians. Where is he?"

"Oh…well…he's kind of with a guardian right now…transported against his will by a glowing orb of light." Brayden chuckled nervously as Tayren walked back to his desk. He smashed his fists down on the desktop.

"He's probably already dead by now!" Tayren said with a despondent look on his face. Then he glanced up at a picture of himself with two children above the mantelpiece. Then he nodded, hoping it wasn't too late, and turned back to Brayden. "Go find him! Guards!"

Two guards anxiously ran into the room.

"Accompany him to find the Chosen One. I can only hope he's still alive. We can't continue our quest without him. I'll keep training the other guards and warriors in preparation for hopeful battle."

"Wait, so much is happening at once!" Brayden said before the guards grabbed him. "Look, my name's Brayden, and—"

"I don't care who you are. Find my Chosen One!"

Ratchet returned to his kingdom completely distraught after Inferno had murdered Clayton. Ratchet was filled with rage and wondered what he could have possibly done to save Clayton. But the whole trial had taken him by surprise, and he didn't have time to think straight. Suddenly, it hit Ratchet that he could have mentioned Gypsy during the trial and maybe saved Clayton, but his nerves had gotten the better of him. Inferno's words about this being his last warning echoed through Ratchet's mind, and the scar on his neck from Inferno's burning hand glowed red as a reminder of his actions, but Ratchet was still determined to make things as right as he could, and he raced out of his kingdom to confront Gypsy.

***

Gypsy always had a plan, as he could see into the future. He knew Ratchet was on his way to stop him, but instead of running or hiding, he remained seated on his rug inside the Lucky Ore Cavern, ready for the future to become the present. He looked around the room admiring the glow of the yellow ore lighting up the cave walls, appreciating everything about the beautiful energy of the world. He took it all in, like it would be his last chance.

"You're in trouble now!" Ratchet yelled as he came into view. He was full of so much pain and anger after what Inferno had done. "I overheard your conversation with Witch, and I know what you're trying to do. You can't let him be king! You can't stop the guardians! We're all too powerful. We were chosen!"

"Oh, Ratchet. Please, make yourself at home! Would you like some tea?"

"What is this?" Ratchet asked, confused.

"You know, my son *will* be king. There is nothing that can be done about this; his future is bright. Your future on the other hand…well…good luck with that, my friend."

"They say you can see into the future, but I don't believe it!"

"Then how do I know your closest friend was just killed by Inferno and that Gizzy is close to making it to Higher Rank in his quest to put an end to the guardians?"

"How do you know all that?"

"The same way I know Gizzy will open the Prophecy. I told you, I can see the future."

Gypsy laughed, then Ratchet revealed the ace up his sleeve—he was carrying Clayton's explosives.

"Wait! What are you doing with those!?"

"Since you can see into the future so well, you must know that my best friend loved explosives. The second I destroy this cavern and get you away from its protective powers, I'll teleport you to Cloud Temple, where you'll be put on trial, and your whole plan will come to an abrupt end! Bet you didn't see that coming, old one!" Ratchet had a crazed look in his eyes as he readied the explosives. Then he laughed and threw them deep into the cave. He quickly grabbed Gypsy to pull him out of the cavern.

"Oink, oink!" Gypsy said to Ratchet, confusing him as the seconds ticked down on the explosives, coming ever close to a catastrophic explosion.

"What?"

"Oink, oink. You'll know soon enough. Goodbye." Gypsy shoved Ratchet hard toward the entrance and ran deeper into the cavern. Within a few seconds, the explosives went off, and the cavern collapsed, forcing Ratchet to run the remaining feet and dive to safety in the daylight.

Ratchet had to think. What had happened? Had Gypsy just sacrificed himself to make it look like Ratchet killed him!?

"No…*Noooooooo!*"

Luck really hadn't been on Ratchet's side since Gizzy had arrived in Altered. Now two people were dead because of Ratchet. It was clear that Gypsy had tricked him and Ratchet would surely be tried and dethroned after this mess, if not killed by Inferno or imprisoned by the other guardians. Oh, how could he let this all happen? Unsure of what to do, Ratchet fled back to his kingdom to hide and pretend he had nothing to do with the explosion and Gypsy's death. He hoped to the highest powers that nobody found out about this, especially after what Inferno had done to Clayton— Ratchet didn't even want to consider what his own fate might be.

Far away from the explosion, Gizzy climbed to the top of a hill to see above the trees and spotted Higher Rank. Tall watchtowers and little farms were all around the village located on the other side of the forest, and Gizzy and Benji nodded to each other; they had found their destination. As they walked back down the hill, some black magic hit them from behind, knocking them to the ground. Gizzy got up and saw a strange being in a long waistcoat. The bright yellow tie gave him away, too—it was Witch.

"Hey! Do you mind!?" Gizzy shouted. He was fed up with being bullied.

"Oh, sorry. Didn't see you there."

Gizzy found it strange to be finally seeing the being from his dreams. "You're Witch, aren't you? I've been warned about you."

"Have no fear; I'm no threat. I'm on your side, Gizzy. I'm against the guardians, too." Witch walked up to Gizzy and Benji and held his hand out in a gesture of goodwill.

"The guardians killed my friend," Gizzy said.

"Ah, must have been Inferno, the Fire Guardian. Did you know he looks after the Nether?"

"Yes. I've done my research." Gizzy was annoyed by Witch and decided to ignore his presence and continued to walk toward Higher Rank.

"Hold on, now," Witch said. "Don't go to Higher Rank just yet! You need to wake up the king first, otherwise this visit will be for not."

Gizzy stopped walking, confused, and turned back to face Witch. "What are you talking about? Brayden told me only the Chosen One can wake the king."

"Um, hello!? Anything in that noggin of yours?"

Witch tapped Gizzy on the head, and Gizzy realized that perhaps he really might be the Chosen One. "You're not from this world, came here under odd circumstances, and you've survived quite a lot to get to this point. All of these things just might point to you being the Chosen One, don't you think?"

"How did you know all that?" Gizzy asked.

"Maybe you're not the only one who does his research," Witch said and chuckled. "Look, before heading to Higher Rank, you can go to the Jungle of Hope, really isn't too far from here. You can wake the king with a simple touch, and with the king back, it'll stop the guardians from being...well...guardians!"

Gizzy and Benji looked at each other. Neither of them felt as though they could trust Witch, but even so, he made valid points. They were all against the guardians, and with King Alpha back, the guardians would lose their powers.

Benji shrugged and nodded, confirming they might as well give it a shot. "Gizzy, we've got nothing to lose. It makes sense bringing the king back from the dead first, and maybe it'll work…but maybe it won't. No harm in trying, I guess."

"Yeah, listen to your fairy friend. He knows what he's talking about."

"Well, the Earth Guardian captured me, the Air Guardian betrayed me, the Water Guardian tried to trick me into admitting my truth, and the Fire Guardian killed my friend…so I've got nothing but revenge on my mind at this point. OK, let's put an end to them!"

Gizzy stepped forward and put his hand out. Witch smiled, and they had a long shake.

"We'll need to know how to get there," Gizzy said, and handed over Brayden's compass so Witch could put in the coordinates to the Jungle of Hope.

"Here you go! Oh, and you should have this!" Witch handed Gizzy a pendant with a gold charm at the end of it.

"What is it?"

"The Pendant of Luck. It's made from Lucky Ore, very rare. While wearing it the guardians can't track you. Nobody can track you if you keep this on."

Gizzy put the pendant on and nodded. "Thank you. I truly appreciate your help, Witch."

"Not a problem at all," Witch said.

Gizzy turned and walked away with Benji flying at his side.

And so, Gizzy began yet another new adventure, this time to the Jungle of Hope to hopefully bring King Alpha back from the dead. Gizzy looked over toward Higher Rank and realized that the compass was pointing east of the village, so he nodded in that direction, made a turn, and left Witch in the distance as they went ever forward.

"I'm not sure about this; we were warned about Witch," Benji warily said several minutes later when he was certain Witch couldn't hear him.

Gizzy had heard Benji but ignored him for the moment. *Hope* was the word swirling around in Gizzy's head, representative of his present state of mind, the only thing he could truly count on given his current predicament—hope. So much had happened since he had arrived in Altered, but it was hope that kept driving him toward the future.

Was The Jungle of Hope really the place where he stood the best chance to begin his stand against the guardians? Hope…and the king of Altered would once again claim his place at the top of the mountain.

As Gizzy continued on his new quest, unaware of many events unfolding around him—Ratchet being responsible for the death of Gypsy, Brayden hunting for him with the guards from Higher Rank, the guardians planning to stop Gizzy from getting to the Prophecy any way they were able—all Gizzy could think about was getting home and how great it would feel to return to some kind of normalcy, despite the strange and fantastic adventure he had experienced. Wasn't home the right place for him? Hadn't that always been the goal? Sure, he had questioned it, gone back and forth in his mind, but wasn't home the only place for him? Or was there something more for his life…his future?

So many questions lingered as the duo continued through the Altered world. Why did Brayden leave for Higher Rank without them? What was the connection between the Green Bloods and *LUCK* and whose blood was the word written in? Why did the blond transwolf from the pack hiding in the cave have a magnifying glass on his leg? Did everyone back on Earth believe that Gizzy had died when the cruise ship was torn apart and sank to the ocean floor? And what was this god-forsaken Prophecy, anyway, and why was it so important for Gizzy to reach it? Could Gizzy really be the Chosen One who would save Altered? Or would he fail in this ultimate quest after all the hours and days and challenges he had already faced? Nothing was certain in this world of Altered, and maybe there really was no escape and Gizzy would be left here forever. Any decision he made now would create a ripple effect for the entire future of the planet and every being inside Altered. And Gizzy had to keep reminding himself that he had asked for an adventure for so long and had received it in a big way, though it was no ordinary adventure…this was an altered adventure.

The Jungle of Hope waited for them as Gizzy and Benji flowed through the open world with the dark-red sun setting behind them, unaware that they were being watched from afar. Little did the duo realize that they were being hunted by some familiar faces…

Woof and his pack had discovered the duo, followed them from a great distance, and had been plotting the right moment to stage an attack. The pack hid in the shadows, eager for the sun to fully go down and allow them to transform from Justments into vicious wolves. It was nearly dark.

"Are we ready to strike?" Woof asked the blond Justment as he walked closer, returning from scouting Gizzy and Benji's movements far away. He came out from under the shadows of great trees, a small male with scratches all over his face, tatty blond hair, and…ragged pirate clothes…it was Brandon!

"Yes, Master. I overheard that they were heading to the Jungle of Hope to free the old king from the sleep of death. We can surprise them there!"

Woof put his hand on Brandon's shoulder. "Prepare yourself," he said.

Brandon nodded and went to join the others. As he walked over to the pack, Brandon's ripped pants revealed a magnifying glass tattoo on his leg. Soon the green, misty moon took over the sky of Altered, and the five transwolves agonizingly transformed into violent, wild beasts. The pack howled into the sky, and at Woof's first movement, the wolves ran as fast as they could toward Gizzy and Benji, drool falling from their sharp teeth at the thought of the hunt and tearing apart their helpless prey.

Gizzy and Benji, with hope filling their hearts and minds, marched blissfully unaware toward the Jungle of Hope.

Made in the USA
Lexington, KY
18 April 2017